WALTHAM FOREST LIBRARIES
904 000 00480505

I HAVE NO SECRETS

PENNY JOELSON

First published in Great Britain in 2017
by Electric Monkey, an imprint of Egmont UK Limited
The Yellow Building, 1 Nicholas Road, London W11 4AN

ISBN 978 1 4052 8615 2

The moral rights of the author have been asserted

67155/1

www.egmont.co.uk

A CIP catalogue record for this title is available from the British Library

Typeset by Avon DataSet Ltd, Bidford on Avon, Warwickshire
Printed and bound in Great Britain by the CPI Group

For Michael and Zoe

1

I tense as soon as I hear the doorbell. I know it's him. I know it's Dan. Sarah's still upstairs getting ready and I hope she comes down soon. I don't want him coming in here.

Mum calls up to Sarah and I hear her say she'll be down in a tick. 'We've been keeping her busy, I'm afraid,' Mum tells Dan, 'so she hasn't had much time to get ready!'

'Ah, I know she wouldn't have it any other way,' says Dan. 'She's a diamond – and you too. What you do for these kids.'

I listen to them chatting away and Mum laughing at Dan's jokes. Everyone loves Dan. Then Mum says she must get back to the kitchen, she's left things on the stove and she's sure Sarah won't be long.

It's quiet for a moment. I hear the distant clattering of pans in the kitchen. Then I hear Dan's voice, coming closer as he speaks.

‘What are you watching, then? Ah – *Pointless*!’

I can hear him breathing. Then he whispers, ‘Bit like your life, eh, Jemma?’

He’s standing behind me now, but I can’t see him because my wheelchair is facing the TV. I try to focus on the quiz questions and forget he’s there, but he gives a long, dramatic sigh.

‘Don’t know how you can bear it.’ His voice is low, not loud enough to be overheard. ‘Watching the telly must be the most excitement you get.’ He only speaks like this when no one else is around. He used to ignore me completely, but not any more.

He moves so he is in front of me, blocking my view of the TV. Grimacing, he leans forwards. I get a gulping feeling, a tightness in my throat.

‘If I were you, I’d top myself,’ he whispers.

My heart thuds as he rubs his head thoughtfully.

‘Oh, yeah – you can’t, can you? Listen,’ he continues, ‘if you ever want a bit of help, I could –’

We both hear footsteps on the stairs. Dan backs away. His face transforms from ugly sneer to fake grin, his features softening as if they have been remoulded.

‘I’d have done better than that pair!’ he laughs,

pointing to the telly. 'Reckon we should go on this, eh, Sarah?'

I get a waft of Sarah's perfume, which is quickly overtaken by the smell of onions frying in the kitchen.

'I'm useless at quizzes,' she laughs as she comes into view. 'I bet Jemma could do it, though, if she had the chance.'

I don't know about that, although I do sometimes get the right answers. It's possible I'd be better than Sarah. She's a brilliant carer, but she's not too clever when it comes to general knowledge – or boyfriends.

At the edge of my vision, I see her kiss Dan softly on the lips.

Watching them, my own mouth feels suddenly dry.

The pair playing *Pointless* are out. They look very disappointed.

Dan and Sarah only have eyes for each other. 'Ready?' Dan smiles at Sarah. 'You look stunning, babe.'

She nods and turns to me. Her eyes are sparkly, her cheeks flushed. 'Bye, Jem. See you in the morning.'

'See you, Jemma,' says Dan. He winks at me.

2

'Sorry to leave you so long, pet!'

Mum bundles into the room and I'm relieved to hear her warm, soft voice. She switches off the telly and pushes my wheelchair into the kitchen, to my place at the end of the table.

I hear the car on the drive. Dad's back from taking Finn to his swimming lesson and picking up Olivia from ballet. Soon the kitchen is noisy and cheerful, as usual, and I push Dan out of my mind.

Olivia's boasting to Mum about how good her dancing was and I watch as she shows Mum the new steps, while Mum tries to get her to sit down at the table. She's nine and has only been here a year. We're all fostered – I've been here since I was two and so has Finn, who's nearly six. I've heard Mum say Olivia was 'hard to place'. Maybe that goes for Finn and me too, though Olivia's problems are different from ours. Finn is autistic, and right now is lining all his beans up neatly on the plate with his fingers. He's obsessed with straight lines. Olivia's a whirlwind – sometimes a tornado – and she's loud. Finn and I don't speak, so life is very different and much noisier since she came.

'Sit down, Olivia!' Dad says in his 'firm but kind' voice, and Olivia finally does. At least she doesn't start one of her tantrums.

Mum serves up Dad's shepherd's pie and beans then starts feeding me my mushed-up version. Dan's words creep back into my head while I'm eating and I try to shut them out.

'*If I were you, I'd top myself. Listen, if you ever want a bit of help, I could –*'

I can't believe he said it – as if my life is worth nothing!

Olivia is wolfing down her food like she's never eaten before. She's skinny, but she has a huge appetite. Finn isn't eating. He's still lining up his beans, concentrating as if his life depends on it.

'Come on, Finn,' Dad coaxes. 'Time to eat them now.'

But Finn clearly doesn't think his line is straight enough.

'Finn, my love,' says Mum gently, 'why don't you start with the pie?'

I don't think Finn is listening to Mum, but I think he's happy now with his line of beans. In any event, he forks a small amount of shepherd's pie into his mouth.

Mum spoons some more into mine.

'I saw Paula earlier,' she tells Dad. 'She looks dreadful, the poor woman.'

'Still no news, then?' Dad asks.

Mum shakes her head.

'News about what?' Olivia demands.

Paula lives down the road, and her son, Ryan, was murdered last month. He was nineteen and he was stabbed to death and no one knows who did it. Everyone's talking about it, though – it's even been on the radio.

Dad quickly changes the subject.

'Finn's swimming like a fish now,' he tells Mum. 'He's come on so fast.'

'And I was really good at ballet!' Olivia says, never wanting to be left out.

'I'm sure you were,' says Dad.

'How was school?' Mum asks Olivia.

Olivia shrugs.

Olivia never wants to talk about school. It's like it's some big secret for her.

I have no secrets of my own. I've never done anything without someone knowing about it. I'm fourteen years old and I have severe cerebral palsy. I am quadriplegic, which means I can't control my arms or legs – or anything else. I can't eat by myself. I can't go to the loo without help. I can't move without someone lifting me with a hoist or pushing me in a wheelchair. I also can't speak.

I've been this way all my life. I can see, though, and I can hear, and sometimes people forget that; they don't realise that I have a functioning brain. Sometimes people talk about me as if I'm not even there. I hate that.

And sometimes people tell me their secrets. I think it's because it's quite hard to hold a one-way conversation. If they are alone with me, they want to talk to pass the time and they end up telling me stuff. They know I won't tell anyone else so they think telling me is safe. The perfect listener.

Sarah told me her secret. She's cheating on Dan. She's still seeing Richard, her old boyfriend, because he's so sweet and she can't bear to hurt him by breaking up with him. Neither of them knows the other exists.

I'm always worried when Sarah has a boyfriend,

although I enjoy the way she gossips to me about them. She has this dream of a fairy-tale wedding – she's even shown me pictures of her ideal wedding dress online. I know I should want her to be happy – and I do. It's just that I'd miss her so much if she went off to get married. She's the best carer I've had.

More than that, I don't want her to marry someone who isn't good enough for her. And I definitely don't want her going off to marry Dan.

3

Sarah's in a great mood when she's back on duty the next morning, though I can tell she's got a hangover and is trying to hide it. She's drinking loads of coffee. She clearly had a good night out with Dan and is singing a track by our favourite band, Glowlight.

She's wheeling me from my bedroom to the kitchen when I hear the clunk of post landing on the mat. Sarah stops to pick it up and puts the small pile of letters on the kitchen table.

'Oh look – one for you, Jemma,' she comments. As she pushes me into my place, I see that the top letter, though addressed to Mum and Dad, has my name on it too – *Parents/guardians of Jemma Shaw*. I rarely get post. I wonder what it could be?

Mum picks up the pile and glances down. Then she quickly moves my letter to the bottom and puts them all on the kitchen counter. Sarah doesn't seem to notice.

Now I am even more curious. Why doesn't Mum want to open it?

After breakfast Sarah goes to get Olivia ready and Dad gets up to leave for work. Mum follows him out into the hallway to kiss him goodbye. Their voices are muffled, but I can pick out Mum's words. She says, 'There's been another letter. I haven't read it yet, but I think we'll have to tell her.'

I strain to hear Dad's reply. 'Yes – she is family. Jemma has a right to know.'

Family? What are they talking about? If only I could ask. It sounds like they're planning to tell me. I just have to hope that they do.

Dad's gone and Sarah's in the kitchen with me, easing my arms gently into my coat, ready for school. I'm conscious that my letter is still there, at the bottom of the pile on the counter.

Olivia's moaning that she can't find her reading book.

Mum sighs. 'When did you last have it, Olivia?'

Olivia shrugs. 'Dunno.'

'Have a look in your bedroom, will you?' Mum tells her.

Olivia slopes off slowly towards the stairs.

'Sarah, can you go with her? I can't see it down here.'

'Sure,' says Sarah. 'You're ready, Jemma. That's one down at least!' She hurries off after Olivia.

'Where's Finn's water bottle?' Mum mutters to herself. 'I'm sure I washed it yesterday. I bet you know where I put it, Jemma.'

As it happens, I do know. I saw it fall off the draining board and down behind the bin.

The doorbell rings and Mum wheels me towards the door. We never know if it will be my minibus or Finn's cab that comes first. Today it's the cab that takes Finn to his special school.

Mum sighs and pushes a spare green water bottle into Finn's bag, which is not going to please Finn as he always has the blue one. She helps him with his coat and gives his hair a quick comb. He wriggles away as fast as he can and out the front door with his taxi escort, Jo.

'Reading book found,' Sarah says, coming down the stairs.

'I hope you said thank you, Olivia?' says Mum, though she knows full well that Olivia hasn't.

'It wasn't me who lost it, Lorraine!' Olivia protests. 'Why do you always have a go at me? It's not my fault!'

She stamps her feet and I'm relieved when the doorbell rings again so I can leave before Olivia starts screaming.

But all I think about as the minibus jolts along the road is the letter. I try to work out what Mum and Dad were talking about. Family? Mum has an aunt and Dad has a brother, but we don't see much of them as they live a long way from here. Were they talking about their family? Or . . . or could it be *mine* – like my natural mum, the one who gave birth to me and then dumped me? Could she have finally decided she wants to see me?

I hope it's not her. I don't want to see her – not ever! She probably only wants to get a look at me and gawp. I hope Mum and Dad tell her to get lost.

As soon as Dad is back in the evening I am waiting for them to talk to me – but they don't say anything. I couldn't even see my letter in the kitchen at dinner time. The whole pile had gone. Have they changed their minds or are they waiting for Finn and Olivia to be in bed, so they can talk about it? I'm not exactly looking forward to a conversation about my birth mum, but waiting for it and wondering about it is even worse.

Dad washes up while Mum and Sarah put Finn and Olivia to bed. It seems like it takes forever, even though I know it is probably just the normal amount of time. But then, finally, when it's nearly my bedtime and I'm watching TV on my own, Mum and Dad both come in. Mum pauses the TV and Dad turns me round to face the sofa and sits down, looking serious.

He has the letter in his hand. I get a surge of relief mixed with panic.

'We've got something to tell you, Jemma,' he says gently. 'Something important.'

My heart is beating so fast. Suddenly I don't want to hear – I don't want to know.

'We've had a letter,' Dad continues, 'from social services.' He pauses, as if unsure how to carry on.

Mum sits down beside him. 'Jemma, I know this is going to be a bit of a shock and I will explain why we haven't told you before . . .'

I wait.

Dad reaches out and touches my hand. 'You've got a sister, Jemma.'

What?

A sister?

Mum sighs and smiles. 'Her name's Jodi.'

I try to take it in. The shock is making me breathless. A sister. I was so sure it was my birth mum wanting to see me. A *sister* – a sister is something completely different.

'The thing is,' Mum continues, 'we knew she wasn't told about you. So we thought it might be upsetting for you to know about her. But she found your name mentioned in some papers and . . . I'm sorry, Jemma. It's been hard to know what to do.'

They knew! All this time Mum and Dad have known that I have a sister. So many feelings are swirling round inside me. The thought of them not telling me makes me angry – but Mum's right. It would have been hard knowing about her if she was never going to know about me. I am still in shock, but I'm curious too.

A sister. My sister. I start to wonder what she's like – how old she is . . .

'The papers Jodi found, they were her adoption

papers,' Mum continues. 'You and Jodi were split up when you were taken into care. Your natural mum couldn't cope – she had a lot of problems. She was very young, and on her own.'

I've sometimes imagined it – my mum giving me up. I could even picture her face, horrified at her own baby, unable to cope with what I was. But there were two of us – two children. That idea never entered my head. And she couldn't look after my sister either. Is my sister disabled too? I'm not sure what to make of this – but I know it changes things. It changes everything.

'Jodi's been asking if she can . . . contact you,' says Dad, drawing me out of my thoughts.

I get a surge of excitement that quickly sinks when I think what they would have had to tell Jodi – that I can't exactly contact her back.

'She's been persistent, but we weren't sure if it was a good idea,' says Mum. 'It's so hard when you can't tell us how you feel about it. . . . But we've told her about you, and we've said she can write to you. I hope it's what you want, Jemma. I really do.'

My sister! I'm still finding it hard to believe that I have one. I wonder how much she's been told about me. Will she really want to know me once she finds out what I'm like? I am thrilled, though. I can't wait to know more about her. She's going to write to me! My sister is going to write to me!

4

'I still can't believe you've got a sister and no one told you!' Sarah exclaims, as she picks up a book to read to me in bed. 'I knew nothing, Jemma. Your mum and dad never even mentioned her.'

I definitely believe her – if Mum and Dad had told Sarah about Jodi she'd have let something slip. She'd never keep something like that from me.

'Me and my sister Kate,' says Sarah, 'we don't always get on, but I can't imagine growing up and not knowing her. I bet you can't wait for a letter from Jodi!'

Sarah keeps mentioning Jodi over the next couple of days. It's like she's as excited as I am. I wish I could tell her how nervous it makes me, though. What if Jodi doesn't write?

At least it means Sarah's not talking about Dan so much. I can almost start to pretend he doesn't exist. In fact, today Sarah isn't talking at all – she's concentrating as she battles to get my rebellious arms into the sleeves of a jumper. My muscle spasms are worse than usual because I've not been sleeping well. Thinking about my sister has been keeping me awake.

'Tonight's the night,' she whispers. I wonder what she means. She's not seeing Dan again, is she? She's seeing so much of him I'm scared sometimes that she's going to run off with him! But of course, she'd never do that.

'I'm splitting up with Richard,' she says. 'It has to be done – I'm not being fair on him.' She runs a brush quickly but gently through my short tangly hair. 'I can't keep putting it off. I know he'll be gutted, though – he's such a softy.'

At last Sarah is doing the right thing. It's no good going out with someone just because you feel sorry for them. Now she just needs to dump Dan too! I wish she had more sense with men. She's had a few boyfriends since she's been here and they've all been hopeless. Like Jason, who was always borrowing money from her and never giving it back, and a guy called Mario who was only interested in football and a total bore. Next was wimpy Richard. And then Dan came along.

*

Sarah's in her room getting ready to go out when the doorbell rings. She's meeting Richard in town, so I know it's not him. I'm in the living room, but the door's open and for once I'm at an angle where I can see into the hall. Dad opens the front door. I hear Dan's voice greeting him.

What's *he* doing here? Sarah is definitely not expecting him.

Dad invites Dan in and I hear the front door shut, then I watch them as they chatter about the weather. When Dan sees Sarah all dressed up, what's he going to think? He'll get suspicious for sure. I strain to listen, but now Olivia's started one of her tantrums. She's lying on the floor somewhere behind me, kicking and screaming like a two-year-old except twice as loud.

I hear Dad call upstairs, 'Sarah! Dan's here!'

He's assumed Sarah's going out with Dan tonight!

At least he's warned her – it would be awful if she came down and just found Dan in the hall. I have no idea what she's going to do.

Thankfully Dan doesn't come into the living room – I think Olivia's screaming has put him off. Mum comes in to see what's up with her, saying a quick hello to Dan as she passes. She turns my wheelchair round, which is annoying as I'd rather watch what's happening in the hall than look at Olivia, who is lying on the floor at the far end of the room, pointing and screaming. Now I can see what's upset her. One of her ballet shoes is trapped on the candelabra light fitting, near the ceiling. Finn must have thrown it up there. He's got good aim.

Mum calms Olivia and says Dad will get it down. Finn is nowhere to be seen. Mum turns me to face the TV and switches it on. Then she pulls Olivia up gently, hugging her, and holds her hand to lead her out. I hear them going upstairs.

I'm conscious that Dan is still in the hall. Sarah calls to say she'll be down in a few minutes. Then I hear Dan sigh. He walks into the room and goes straight to the telly and picks up the remote, flicking through channels. He's acting as if I'm not even here. I wish I could say, 'Oi! I was watching that!' even though I wasn't really.

He settles on the news. I don't want the news. On the screen I can see a coffin being carried into a church. A reporter is speaking. It's only when I hear him say the name Ryan Blake that I start paying attention properly.

Ryan – from down the road. It was his funeral today. I want to know what the police have found out. Mum and Dad think Ryan might have been into drugs.

'Police are still appealing for witnesses,' the reporter continues, 'and his parents are pleading for anyone who knows anything to come forward.'

Dan suddenly turns towards me.

'You don't know anything . . . do you, our Jemma?' he sniggers.

I can't bear him calling me 'our Jemma', like he's part of the family or something.

'Here's a secret for you,' he continues, 'and I know you won't go telling anyone.' He winks. There's a pause. He presses his face close to mine, so close I can feel his hot breath on my cheeks. 'They're never gonna catch me!' he whispers, screwing up his eyes and then nodding at the screen. He stands back, smiling, as if he's gloating. 'There's something for you to chew on, *freak*!'

Sarah's feet patter on the stairs.

Dan quickly flicks the channel over to a game show.

Catch him? What did he mean?

It's a wind-up – it must be . . .

'Hiya, babe,' he says.

'What are you doing here?' Sarah asks. I see her arms flapping a bit like Finn. I can tell she's panicking, but she's also gazing longingly into Dan's eyes. She won't cancel on Richard to go out with Dan, will she? She needs to split up with *both* of them. I wish she could hear what I'm telling her in my head.

'You left a glove in my car,' he tells her. 'I only found it today. I was passing so I thought I'd pop it in. Don't want you getting chilly fingers!'

'Oh, thanks! I was wondering where it was,' she replies. 'But I've got to get a move on. I'm off out with Emma and Rihanna – we're going to the cinema.'

'Out again?' he says.

'Yes, I switched my next night off. It's Emma's birthday,' Sarah says quickly. Sarah seems to have her excuse ready prepared – but I guess this is what she's told Mum. 'We're having a girls' night out. Becks is coming too. We're seeing that film you said was for soppy teenage girls.'

'No way!'

'Yeah, really.' Sarah laughs for a little too long. 'And I've gotta go or I'll be late.'

'No worries, I'll give you a lift,' says Dan.

'No, Dan. I'm fine,' Sarah assures him.

'It's no prob,' says Dan.

'Oh . . . All right, then.'

An uneasy feeling grips my chest. I don't want her to go with him. What he said to me . . . Surely he was joking. Dan's horrible, but he wouldn't actually kill someone. Would he? And why did he turn up here this evening? It doesn't feel right. Maybe she's done something to make him suspicious. Was he trying to catch her out?

Sarah says goodbye to me and touches my hand gently. Her hand is hot – she knows this is a mess and she briefly meets my eyes with a look that says she knows I know this too. She turns to the door.

'Bye, Jemma,' Dan says, winking again. I see his sneering face in my head when he called me *freak* and remember what else he said. I don't trust him one bit.

They go and I hear the front door bang shut.

Dad comes in and stares up at the ballet shoe on the light fitting, muttering, 'You've got to be joking,' under his breath.

5

Mum gets me ready for bed, but I'm barely listening as she chats away about needing to get me some new clothes. What did Dan mean?

If only Mum could see inside my head – the thoughts spinning round. But I know on the outside I must look exactly the same as I always do. Nothing shows. No one knows.

He must have been joking. If he was involved then wouldn't we have heard something? Wouldn't he be a suspect? Even so, I wish I could tell someone. Just so they can know what he's like. Just in case.

If he *was* confessing, then he knew he was telling the one person who would keep his secret safe. Maybe he thinks I don't even understand what he says. I just want to know for sure. Because if Dan is a murderer, and he finds out Sarah is cheating on him . . .

I can't sleep at all, waiting to know that Sarah is safely back. My room is downstairs, but at the back of the house, and I listen for the sound of the front door. Finally I hear her come in, but I'm facing away from my bedside clock so can't see the time. Maybe she'll come in to turn me – I have to be turned in the night so I don't get sore from being in one position. Yes. I can hear her footsteps.

She's breathing quite fast and her hands aren't as gentle as usual. She catches my eye in the dimmed light, and sees that I'm awake. I will her to tell me what happened. Sometimes Sarah seems to read my mind. That's one of the things I love about her.

'That wasn't the best evening of my life,' she whispers.

I wait eagerly for more. She sits down on the edge of the bed.

'I can't believe Dan turned up! That glove thing was just an excuse, don't you think? He's getting so serious – he said he couldn't bear to be apart from me.' She laughs. 'I sat in his car with my fingers crossed that he wouldn't think something was wrong. Then he wanted to actually come into the cinema with me, but luckily it was really hard to park so he couldn't.'

She runs her hand through her hair. Only Sarah would get herself into this situation.

'I was scared he might hang around so I texted Richard from the loos to say I'd be late and waited ten minutes before I even dared walk to the pub! You've gotta laugh, Jem.'

Sarah is not taking this seriously at all. At least it sounds like Dan didn't catch her out.

'When I got there,' she continues, 'Richard looked so pleased to see me. I just couldn't do it to him.'

My heart sinks. Sarah is fidgeting and looks excited about something. Has she changed her mind and decided she wants to be with Richard after all?

'Jem, he's only gone and booked tickets for us to see Glowlight next month! It'll be amazing!' She gives me a sheepish look. 'Is it really bad if I keep going out with him until then?'

Glowlight! Well, it's not great to use him for his tickets, but it is *Glowlight*. Maybe I'd do the same . . . No, this is wrong. Sarah needs to break up with Richard!

'Perhaps we could just go to the concert as friends,' she continues. 'But I don't think Richard would like that. I know Dan wouldn't.'

She sighs and smooths my duvet down.

'I'm such a coward, Jem.'

I don't know what I'd do if I were Sarah – though I'd like to think I wouldn't get myself into such a mess in the first place.

6

When the minibus drops me back from school on Monday, Mum tells me we have visitors. She pushes my wheelchair into the kitchen, where Mr and Mrs Blake are drinking tea. Paula and Mum have known each other for years, but more to say hello in the street than as actual friends. I remember her coming to Mum a few times when Ryan was young and playing up, asking Mum for advice. I think there was a time when she even hoped Mum would foster him.

Since Ryan died Mum's tried to be supportive, and Paula's been round here a few times. Graeme – Mr Blake – doesn't usually come with her, though.

Paula says hi to me and smiles, but her grief is clear in the deep lines on her face and her drooping eyes. Graeme shuffles awkwardly and taps the rim of his mug with his finger. I can tell that I make him uncomfortable. I notice he's kept his black outdoor jacket on while Paula has taken off her coat.

He's clearly hoping not to be here long.

'I know he was no angel,' Paula is saying to Mum, 'but I was so hard on him – always nagging, criticising, going on at him to change. The last thing I said to him was, "Get out and don't come back!" Can you believe it? That's what I said!'

She bursts into tears.

Graeme touches her shoulder and shuffles awkwardly again.

Mum hands Paula a tissue.

'I know,' says Mum, 'but you could never have known what would happen. You were trying to set boundaries. He knew you loved him. He knew that's why you kept on at him.'

'Do you really think so?' Paula sobs.

When we were little, Ryan used to stick his tongue out at me if he passed me in the street. Then when he got a bit older, he called me 'Spaz' or 'Spazzie' or worse things. He even spat at me once.

I don't miss Ryan, but obviously I feel horrible for Paula. Ryan was a loser, but he was still her son – and Graeme's.

I look at Graeme. He's like a block of stone.

Paula sips her tea. 'I can't bear the thought that the

monster who did it is walking around free. I might pass him in the street and never know.'

Dan's face comes into my mind. *Yes, you might*, I think. *He was here – he was here in this house*, I want to tell Paula. A sound comes out of my mouth, a strained gurgle. Paula glances at me and quickly away again.

I wish I could tell them what he said. Just in case. I don't know if Dan and Ryan even knew each other. They're very different. And Dan doesn't seem like he'd be involved with drugs and gangs and stuff. Or maybe he's just good at hiding it. 'We'd better be off,' Graeme says gruffly.

Paula turns and gives him a bewildered look as if to say, 'Off where? Off for what? What is there to be off for?'

But she pulls herself up from the chair and Graeme helps her on with her coat.

'At least the *Crimewatch* thing might help,' I hear Mum say, as she sees them out. 'Let's just hope someone calls in and the police get a lead.'

So Ryan's murder is going to be on *Crimewatch*! Maybe that will make everything clear. I hope Mum and Dad will let me watch it. I've never seen it, but I know about it – how they reconstruct crimes, and people watching can phone up if they know anything. Maybe there will be some clue that will tell me if Dan really did it – and if he did, then Sarah or Mum or Dad or someone else watching will surely realise it was him.

7

Sarah greets me when the minibus drops me back from school on Tuesday, with a smile even bigger than her usual cheerful one.

'Ooh, Jem! A letter's come from your sister! Your mum hasn't opened it. She's waiting for you. But I hope she'll show me later! I'm dying to know what she's said.'

Sarah wheels me into the kitchen, announcing 'Jemma's home!' to Mum. She doesn't go – I think she's hoping Mum will let her stay.

'Thanks, Sarah,' says Mum.

Sarah shoots me a pretend annoyed look and leaves, closing the door after her.

We sit at the kitchen table and Mum carefully opens the white envelope.

My heart thuds.

'Are you ready for this?' Mum asks.

She puts the letter down so I can see it.

'Dear Jemma,' she reads. *'I didn't know you existed until a few months ago. I found some papers in a drawer that were about me. One of them had your name on it under mine. My name is Jodi and I am your sister!'*

Mum pauses and looks up at me, before continuing.

'In fact, more than that, Jemma. We are twins!'

Twins? Mum never told me that.

'We must have been born only minutes apart,' Mum reads. *'The thing is – I've always had this weird feeling – like something was missing. When I found out about you I thought – this is it! This explains it. I have a twin sister. We spent nine months together before we were born and we've been separated ever since.'*

Missing? I've never felt that. But maybe that's because so much else is missing for me – like legs and arms that work and a voice.

Mum is still reading.

'Now I'm going to tell you some stuff about me. I live in Enfield – only a few miles from you! I live with my mum and dad (the ones who adopted me), but I don't have any brothers or sisters. I've ALWAYS wanted a sister.

'Favourite things. Colour – purple. Food – ice-cream

sundae. Sport – hockey (I play for the school team). Pet – cat (mine's called Fluff – she really is like a fluffy white bundle and I love her to bits! She went missing last year and was found up a tree after three days!). People – my best friend, Ava, my boyfriend, Jack, and my parents too. They are lovely and even though I was angry that they didn't tell me about you and they were upset that I found out, they've calmed down now and said they're sorry that they didn't tell me before.

'There's so much more I could write, but I'll stop now as I've got tons of homework.

'I know you have disabilities and that you can't write back. I've been told about that. It's no big deal. Don't worry, I'll keep writing!

'I've put in a photo of me, though our printer at home is rubbish and it's come out a bit dark. I'll try to find a better photo – and maybe next time I'll send you a picture of Fluff too!

'I will write again soon.

'Love, Jodi x.'

Mum holds the photo so I can see it. It's kind of blurry, but Jodi has dark hair like mine and her eyes are a bit like mine too. She looks pretty.

'I'll reply for you, Jemma,' says Mum. 'And I'll

encourage Jodi to keep writing. We'll take things slowly and hopefully one day you'll be able to meet her.'

I'm only half listening. I can't take my eyes off the photo. That's my sister – my twin sister!

Mum puts the photo by my bed and looking at it and thinking about the letter keeps me happy for the next couple of days. I am sleeping better too. It is almost enough to stop me thinking about Dan. But when Thursday evening comes I am desperate for Dad to let me stay in the lounge to watch *Crimewatch*.

Sarah's upstairs putting Finn and Olivia to bed and Mum's getting her coat on to go to Weightwatchers. She's been trying to eat healthily, but I know her secret – I see her hide bars of chocolate between the books on the highest shelf in the lounge.

I'm hoping my limbs stay still and no sounds escape my mouth so she'll forget I'm here as Dad is more likely to let me watch *Crimewatch* than Mum. But Mum comes to say goodbye to me and then turns to Dad.

'I'm not sure Jemma should see it,' she says. 'It might upset her.'

'She's fourteen,' says Dad. 'I bet she'd be interested to see it, wouldn't you, Jemma?' He turns to me and back to Mum. 'It's not as if she hasn't heard us all talk about it.'

I wish I could hug Dad.

Mum still looks uncertain. She glances from Dad to me and back again.

Please!

'All right, then,' says Mum. 'Hopefully I'll be back in time, but if not you'll have to fill me in.'

When it starts, I'm disappointed that Sarah isn't here – but Dad calls her, and she brings a basket of washing in with her to fold, and sits on the armchair.

Mum gets back just as they start showing Ryan's case and she hurries in, still in her coat.

'Put on two pounds,' she sighs, and I hear the sofa creak as she sits down next to Dad.

'Four weeks ago,' the presenter says, 'nineteen-year-old Ryan Blake was brutally stabbed to death in Walden Cross. The culprit and motive remain a mystery. Witnesses have helped to make the reconstruction that you are about to see.'

They show actors, including one I can clearly see is meant to be Ryan, drinking in a local pub, the Hare and Hound. Then Ryan and his friends leave and gradually split up until Ryan is left with one friend, who then heads off for home. Instead of going home himself, Ryan doubles back. No one knows why he did this. He heads down a side street, though they're not sure which one he actually went down – and comes out somewhere behind the station.

That was where his body was found.

'Did you see Ryan in Warduff Street or Mackenzie Avenue between 11 p.m. and midnight?' the presenter asks. 'A man in a black jacket was seen walking along Mackenzie Street just before 11 p.m. This man has not yet been identified. Are you that man or did you also see him that night?'

I try to think like Poirot. I've listened to loads of Agatha Christie audiobooks that Mum's aunt gave me. I need to be observant – to have an eye for anything that might be a clue, even if it seems unlikely. Everyone is a suspect in Agatha Christie. Ryan's friends seem like a dodgy bunch. Maybe the last friend he was with didn't go home. Maybe he doubled back too. Perhaps Ryan had lied to him – or one of the others, or ripped them off. But there isn't much to go on to work out a motive.

What about the man in the black jacket? Dan has a black jacket, but it's a bit different to the one they showed.

Suddenly I remember Graeme – Ryan's dad – sitting in our kitchen. His jacket looked like the one on the programme. Graeme? Is it possible? Could he have got so fed up with Ryan that he lost his temper and killed him? One of the crime books I listened to said most people are killed by members of their families. And in Agatha Christie it's often the quiet ones you have to watch. But Graeme? Murder his own son? It's easier to believe that Dan did it. I've seen what he can be like – even though no one else has.

I want to see Sarah's reaction, but I'm facing the telly. I wish she'd say something.

'Police say the alley behind the station is known to be used by drug dealers,' the presenter continues, 'but no drugs were found in Ryan's blood.' They mention that the knife used hasn't been found and they give the number for people to call.

'Right, Jemma,' says Mum. For a moment I imagine her keying in the number and handing me the phone so I can tell them what Dan said. But of course, she's just telling me that it's time for me to go to bed.

Sarah wheels me out as *Crimewatch* moves on to a series of armed burglaries in Dartford.

8

'Listen, pet, I've got something to tell you,' Mum says the next evening.

I'm all ears – wondering if it's to do with *Crimewatch*. No one's mentioned it since yesterday and I've been waiting for news. Did anyone call the programme? Do the police have any new leads?

Then I wonder if it's Jodi. Has she written again?

'You remember I told you about Carlstone College?' Mum says. 'I've arranged for us to go up there next week.'

My mind whirls – this is so far from what I was thinking about. *Carlstone College*. When Mum talked about it before, she said I might go there when I'm older – not *now.* Has she changed her mind?

'They have a communications expert coming,' Mum tells me. 'Professor Spalding. It's a meeting for any interested families – even those whose children aren't at the college. I can't make any promises – but maybe he'll be able to help you. And we can have a look around too, just to see what it's like.'

A while ago they showed me this leaflet for Carlstone. Mum said they had amazing facilities and might be able to help me much more than the school I'm at. I liked the sound of the college. I thought I might really enjoy it and they do loads more subjects there. Then Mum told me it's a three-hour drive from here. I'd have to live there, like at a boarding school.

Mum said if I went there she and Dad would come and visit, and I'd be able to come home some weekends and in the school holidays. I was so relieved the next day when Mum said she thought I was too young, and maybe some time in the future we'd all go and have a look at it. But I thought that meant in a couple of years – not a couple of months.

And what about Sarah? If she came with me it wouldn't be so bad, but I bet people don't get to take their own carers. And she wouldn't want to be three hours away from Dan, would she?

I try to focus on what Mum is saying about the communications expert. Hopefully our visit really is just about seeing this professor. But I can't stop thinking that it might be something more. The worry is gnawing at my brain, joining the other worries and the questions I can never ask.

I feel myself withdrawing like a tortoise into a shell. Mum's still talking, but I'm no longer listening.

When Sarah comes to fetch me for dinner she looks at me for a moment and frowns.

'What's up, Jem?'

I don't know how she can tell that something's wrong, but she can and I'm glad. Maybe my limbs are even stiffer than usual when she moves me. I certainly feel stiffer. Everything aches.

'I hope you're not coming down with something,' she continues.

She looks into my eyes for clues. I wish they could give her some. She feels my brow, inspects my arms, legs and chest for rashes. Then she gets the ear thermometer and takes my temperature. Hopefully once she's sussed I'm not ill, she'll work out how unhappy I am.

Sarah wheels me into the kitchen. Everyone else is already at the table, but the cutlery is missing. Finn has removed it and lined it all up neatly on the floor against the wall – a row of forks, then knives, then spoons.

Dad shakes his head at Finn and sighs as he picks them up, and there is a delay while he washes them in the sink. He isn't angry. He understands Finn.

'Something's wrong with Jemma,' Sarah tells Mum.

I watch Mum's face. Will she make the connection and realise that what she said before has got me worried?

'Are you hungry?' Mum asks me. 'Sorry dinner's a bit late.'

I'm not hungry. And now I feel sick at the thought of eating.

Sarah shakes her head. 'It's more than that.'

Mum shrugs rather dismissively, and then I wonder if maybe she doesn't want Sarah to know about her plans, because Sarah will lose her job if I'm sent away.

Once the cutlery is washed and dried, Sarah spoons food into my mouth. I find it hard to swallow. Olivia knocks her cup over – I'm not sure if it is accidental or on purpose, but water spreads in a pool across the table and Dad's 'Oh, Olivia' is enough to start her wailing theatrically. Dad tells her to calm down, which brings on a full-blown tantrum. My head is pounding now.

Mum and Dad are both fussing over Olivia. I

scream inside my head sometimes – making the kind of noise she's making now, but of course no one ever knows.

Sarah aims another spoonful into my mouth. I cough and splutter. I can't stop coughing. I need a drink. Sarah is distracted, looking at Olivia, and I start to panic. I feel like I can't breathe. It is a moment before she sits me forward in my wheelchair and pats me on the back. She holds the straw to my lips and looks from me to Mum as Olivia finally stops shrieking. 'I told you something was wrong. I think she's going down with something. I'll sleep in her room tonight.'

No one understands. When I'm worried and I just want reassurance I have no way of getting it. Then my worries just grow and grow. Mum and Dad assume it's something physical because it so often is, but all I want is to be able to tell them how I feel . . .

'Thanks, Sarah,' says Mum. 'There's a nasty fluey bug going round. I hope it isn't that.'

Later, Sarah's getting me ready for bed when her mobile rings.

'It's Dan. We haven't spoken all week. I'd better

answer,' she says apologetically, 'or he might think I'm avoiding him.'

She says hello, and then puts the phone on loudspeaker and leaves it on the bed, crouching to take off my socks. I hear Dan's voice, as clear as if he's in the room.

'How was the film, babe?'

Sarah has taken off one of my socks and started on the other one. She stops, bites her lip and leans towards the phone. 'Great,' she chirps.

'Really? What was so great about it?' he asks.

'Why do you care?' Sarah asks. 'It's not your kind of film – you said so yourself.'

'Just asking,' he says.

There's a pause. 'Sorry,' says Sarah, 'I can't chat now. I'm getting Jemma ready for bed. She's not too well. I'll call you later and tell you all about it, OK?'

'Sure – speak later. Love you, babe!'

Sarah puts her phone in her pocket, then laughs. 'I'll have to look up some reviews online,' she tells me. 'I don't even know who's in it!'

9

'Come on, Finn!' Mum calls cheerfully as we reach the gate of the park.

When I woke up this morning I had this weird floaty feeling, like nothing in my life is real. I am apparently neither ill nor well. It doesn't surprise me that my body's behaving weirdly. All these thoughts have got to get out somehow. Sarah and Mum keep taking my temperature. 'A bit under the weather' is how Mum described me. We often go to the park on Saturdays and she said some fresh air might do me good.

'We'll go and see the ducks first,' Mum tells Finn and Olivia.

If I could roll my eyes, I would. I liked being taken to see the ducks when I was six, but right now I've got other things on my mind. If we have to be here, I was hoping we were going to the park café. It's at the top of the hill and I know it's not easy to push me up there, but from the top you get a view right over the park. I like the feeling of being so high – on top of the world, looking down. From my wheelchair I so often feel low down, looking up at things.

Olivia skips ahead, Sarah's pushing me, and Mum's cajoling Finn – who is walking slowly, flapping his hand in front of his face. I think he likes the patterns of light it makes. Soon we reach the pond and we stop by the barrier, near a clump of early daffodils. I watch Olivia throw corn at the nearest ducks as if she's trying to murder one. I'm sure she just said, 'Yeah! Got it!'

Mum pushes corn into Finn's hand and helps him aim, but the corn just drops on to the path. He isn't really interested and starts to pull away towards the playground.

'OK, Finn, just a minute,' Mum tells him.

Sarah's phone beeps. I bet it's Dan texting her. I see her peeping at it when Mum's not looking. I wish she'd tell me what he said.

When we're in the playground, Sarah wheels me on to the wheelchair-accessible roundabout and pushes the bar gently so it begins to move, before she gets on and stands with me.

'Just a gentle spin today, hey, Jemma?'

This roundabout is here because of my mum; she campaigned for it for years and I was so happy when it arrived. I used to like going fast. It's not often I get to do anything fast. I'm too old for it now, though, and especially not today when my head is already spinning. At least Sarah moves it slowly.

'I'll push!' Olivia says, running up.

'Gently, Olivia,' Sarah tells her. But she's pushing too fast so I'm whirling even faster than the thoughts in my head. I want to stop. I want to get off. Now.

'Olivia! Slow down!' Sarah yells. She leaps off and brings it to a halt.

Olivia rushes away towards the climbing frame.

'Sorry, Jemma! Are you OK?' Sarah asks, touching my shoulder as she pulls the wheelchair off. I feel giddy and breathless. I want to go home. Sarah's phone beeps with another message.

She parks me next to a bench where we can watch Finn on the swing. She turns me carefully to make sure the low sun isn't in my eyes. The swing squeaks noisily. Finn would happily swing for an hour, maybe two, if he was allowed.

Sarah takes out her phone again and reads the new message. I wonder if she managed to convince

Dan that she really went to the cinema.

Olivia runs round, going on everything. She demands that Mum watches her on the monkey bars and then on the climbing wall. She's good at climbing as well as dancing.

I might definitely be too old for playgrounds, but I'd rather be here, with Mum and Sarah and Olivia and Finn, than packed off to some college.

I'm well wrapped in a warm coat and have a blanket over my knees, but I'm starting to feel cold. The fresh air is doing me no good at all, which is no surprise to me. I feel weak and muzzy-headed. The squeaking of the swing is hurting my ears.

Sarah looks up from her phone. 'You're very pale, Jemma.'

She goes over to Mum and asks if she can take me home.

Mum comes and looks at me and nods at Sarah. 'Yes, you guys go – we won't be far behind.'

Sarah pushes me along the pavement, past the local shops, the newsagent's and the barber's.

'Oh, look! See that man coming out of the bookie's?' says Sarah. 'I know him – it's Billy.'

I've heard Sarah call that shop the bookie's,

though I'm not actually sure what they sell. I don't think it's books.

'Hi, Billy!' Sarah calls, as the man walks towards us. The man has his head down, but his shoulders jolt and he looks up sharply, then stops and smiles at her.

'Sarah!' he says. 'You all right?'

Sarah's mentioned Billy – he's a friend of Dan's. She said Dan calls him 'Billy No Brains' which sounded mean to me. Sarah just thought it was funny. My head's really aching now. I hope she's not going to have a long chat with him.

'This is Jemma,' Sarah tells him. 'Jemma, this is Billy.'

Billy comes round in front of me and smiles at me too. He has a big head and his smile's so wide it seems to take up most of his face. But he's a friend of Dan's, so I'm sure he can't be that nice really.

'Hi, Jemma. How ya doing?' says Billy. He looks up at Sarah. 'Dan's well smitten, you know. He don't say much, but I can tell!'

Sarah laughs. 'Really?'

Thanks, Billy, I think crossly. I don't need him telling her that. *Come on, Sarah. Let's go*.

'He's a good bloke, you know. Takes care of his mates. Look, I gotta be off,' says Billy. 'Nice to see you.'

Good.

'I've got to get Jemma home too,' says Sarah. 'She's not well.'

'Say hi to Dan from me,' says Billy. 'Hope you feel better, Jemma.'

10

At last we're home and I'm glad to be inside in the warm. My worries slip away and my head feels better. I enjoy a peaceful five minutes in the lounge before I hear a wailing sound from outside. Mum's key is in the door and the wailing gets louder.

'Come on, inside,' Mum is telling Olivia. I hear Finn run past and up the stairs. I think he finds Olivia's tantrums as painful as I do.

'It wasn't my fault! That boy pushed in front of me!' Olivia blubs.

'You didn't have to hit him, though, did you?' Mum says.

Olivia has thrown herself on the floor and is kicking and screaming at the top of her voice, while Mum tries to calm her down. I wish I could yell and kick like that.

Mum and Olivia eventually go upstairs and the screaming becomes more distant.

By dinner time Olivia's calmed down. I'm still not hungry, though. Sarah realises this when the food she's spooning into my mouth just sits there and doesn't go down.

'Oh, Jem, you're really not well, are you? I'll take your temperature again.'

I don't have a high temperature, which she soon finds out. After dinner, she leaves me in the lounge with Olivia and Finn. They are changed, ready for bed and watching TV in their dressing gowns. They look cosy and cute, curled up either end of the sofa. It's *101 Dalmations* and I'm half watching too, though I'm not really interested. We've seen it loads of times.

Someone's at the front door and I hear Dad go to open it.

And I hear Dan's voice.

He's here *again*.

'I was just passing and I wondered if I could have a quick word with Sarah,' Dan says. 'It won't take long, I promise.'

I wish Dad would just tell him to clear off.

'I'll call her,' Dad says.

Dad leaves Dan waiting in the hall and goes to look for Sarah. But of course Dan doesn't stay there. I hear his breathing as he comes into the living room. I will him to leave me alone.

'Hiya, *Jemma*,' he says.

Olivia jumps and looks up from the telly. Finn's eyes stay firmly fixed on the screen, as if he's heard nothing.

'What are you doing here?' Olivia asks Dan.

'Just popped in to see Sarah,' Dan tells her.

'You're always popping in,' Olivia comments. 'Do you love her?'

I laugh. It comes out as a snort.

I'm curious to see how Dan reacts.

He doesn't answer straight away.

Then, 'Yes, I love her,' he says. He says it like he actually means it.

Olivia giggles. 'D'you wanna see me dance?' she asks.

Dan moves round and I see him nod. 'Go on, then.' He looks longingly at the door. Maybe he wishes he'd stayed in the hall.

Olivia turns off the telly. Finn continues staring at the blank TV screen while she puts on some ballet music. She takes off her dressing gown and begins to dance in her pink pyjamas. Her steps are in perfect time, her toes pointed. Dan claps and she is delighted with the attention.

Then Sarah comes in.

'Dan wanted to see me dance,' Olivia tells her.

'She's good too,' says Dan.

Olivia beams, hanging on to Dan's arm. 'He loves you,' she tells Sarah. 'I know cos he told me.'

Sarah smiles at Dan. 'What's up? It's not the best time . . .'

He untangles himself from Olivia, pulls Sarah into his arms and kisses her – as if that is the answer to her question.

Olivia watches, standing right next to them. She giggles loudly again. 'D'you want me to kiss you like that, Finn?' She flings herself on to the sofa and pushes her lips towards him teasingly. Finn ducks and dashes upstairs.

'Can we go somewhere more private?' Dan asks. 'Only for a minute. I won't keep you from your *work*.'

He heads past me towards the door and I watch anxiously as Sarah follows. She moves quickly out of sight, but I can still hear her in the hallway, telling him we bumped into Billy. They must have moved further away or lowered their voices because I don't hear any more.

Olivia watches them go too and turns to me, her face sullen. She didn't want them to go off to talk 'in private' any more than I did. She starts practising her dance in front of me. I think she's hoping to dance for Dan again before he goes. I hope he goes soon.

I watch Olivia dance. She looks almost angelic with her long wavy blonde hair, loose now after her bath, though usually tied back in a ponytail or plait.

She was in five different foster homes before she came here. *Five!* I can't begin to imagine that. She's lucky Mum and Dad have so much patience and can cope with her.

I hear Sarah and Dan in the hall. And so does Olivia. She stops mid-twirl and dashes out of the room. The front door clicks before she can get there and her screams pierce through the house as she yells at Sarah for not letting her say goodbye to Dan.

It takes Sarah at least five minutes to calm her down. 'Come on, Olivia, time for bed,' Sarah says in the end. I can still hear the occasional muted sob.

My head is pounding from the screaming. Olivia's music is still playing and that doesn't help either.

I sit waiting. The music finally comes to a stop. The house is peaceful at last. I am drifting off. My headache dulls from a throb to a slight pulsing. I'm hoping that when Sarah comes to put me to bed, she'll tell me what Dan said – why he came.

Dad comes in after putting Finn to bed and puts the TV on, turning me so I am facing it.

'*Mastermind*'s on,' he says. 'Let's see how many we can answer.'

The first chosen subject is Agatha Christie. I can actually answer lots of the questions. I even get one right that the man in the chair gets wrong.

Mum comes in eventually and flops down on the sofa next to Dad. Dad puts his arm round her. Mum's mobile rings. Dad sighs as Mum pulls it from her cardigan pocket.

'Hello, Paula,' Mum says. 'How are you, love?' There's a long pause. 'Really? Well that's encouraging!'

'What did she say?' Dad asks, after Mum puts away her phone.

'The police had a lot of calls after *Crimewatch*. Apparently they've been questioning someone today.'

'Let's hope he's the one,' says Dad. 'It would be good to know he's off the streets.'

*

Sarah is unusually quiet as she gets me ready for bed. Most likely Olivia has worn her out. Or maybe it's what Dan said to her in private when he came round. It couldn't have been Dan the police were questioning, could it? Was he telling Sarah he's a suspect? Sarah is quiet, but she doesn't seem shocked or upset. Then again, she's under Dan's spell, like everyone else, so I'm sure he could've convinced her that he had nothing to do with it. I wish she would talk to me.

11

Sarah is still quiet when she dresses me on Sunday morning. She doesn't mention Dan. Mum and Dad say nothing more about Ryan or the man the police questioned. Everyone is busy getting ready for Finn's sixth birthday.

Finn doesn't like balloons, but Dad has found some 'Happy Birthday' bunting with alternating blue and yellow triangles. Finn is oblivious to the specialness of the day, and has no interest in the birthday cards so Olivia opens them for him. Finn is more interested in the coloured envelopes, and proceeds to line them up neatly across the floor. I watch him and at one point he looks up at me and meets my eyes. Although neither of us can speak, I feel close to Finn. I always have. I sense that he likes me watching him.

Mum and Olivia bake a cake. I enjoy the bustle in the kitchen and the lovely baking smells, especially the smell of melted chocolate, which Mum lets me taste from a spoon. Olivia is happy and doing what Mum tells her for a change. Mum is so patient with her, even when she spills a load of sugar on the floor. While the cake's in the oven, Sarah takes Olivia for a walk to the shops and they come back with bags of little sweets and chocolate buttons to decorate it with. Olivia is ecstatic. Once the cake has cooled, Mum ices it with buttercream and Olivia lines up the sweets and chocolate buttons in neat rows saying, 'Finn will like it like that.' She puts the candles in a line across the middle.

'It looks great,' she announces, and rubs her tummy. 'Yum, yum!'

'You'll have to wait until teatime,' Mum warns, but once she's left the room Olivia stays next to the cake, staring at it greedily.

She looks thoughtful, then carefully takes three chocolate buttons and three sweets from each row and moves the others along to cover the gaps. She stuffs the ones she's taken into her mouth.

Mum comes back before Olivia can do it again.

Soon it's time for Finn to open his presents. Dad showed me his present when he bought it and I've been looking forward to seeing Finn's reaction.

We all sit in the living room and watch as Finn opens the stripy wrapping paper parcel. He pulls out a huge box of matchsticks.

They're not matches you light – but ones people use to make model ships with and things like that. There's a picture of one on the box. When Dad showed me I didn't get it at first – I couldn't see Finn making model ships. But then Dad took out a few matchsticks and lined them up. Dad understands Finn.

Finn examines the box, opens it and tips all the matchsticks out. A huge beam spreads across his face. Finn rarely smiles and I have never seen a smile as big as this. I catch Dad's eye – his grin is as big as Finn's. Finn gets busy making a line of matchsticks that stretches the length of the living room.

'Don't give me matchsticks when it's my birthday, will you?' says Olivia.

Dad laughs.

We go into the kitchen and Mum lights the candles on the cake, but Finn is still lining up his matchsticks and won't come in. In the end, Mum brings the cake carefully into the living room and Mum, Dad, Sarah and Olivia sing 'Happy Birthday'. Finn doesn't even look up, but I feel suddenly happy, with the brightness of the candles and the warmth of my family around me.

'You can blow the candles out for him,' Mum tells Olivia, and Olivia jumps up and down with excitement.

We go back to the kitchen to eat the cake, which is delicious, and Mum keeps a piece for Finn to have later.

Two hours after Finn opened the present, he and I are alone in the living room. Finn has moved on from lining the matchsticks up along the wall. He is now arranging them in what looks like a big square around my wheelchair – though I can only see part of it. It definitely has at least two right angles. I sense he is enclosing me completely. Now and then he looks at me and meets my eyes as if seeking my approval. I have never seen Finn make eye contact with anyone apart from me. I like being the centre of his play – I feel alive and connected in a way that is rare for me. I think Finn has completed one square as he is now starting a second one, right around the first. He has never made anything but straight lines before.

I hope Dad will come in – he's going to be so impressed. I hear footsteps, but it's Olivia who comes round in front of me and my heart sinks.

She sometimes messes up Finn's neat lines deliberately and I don't think she'll understand.

She gasps. 'Wow, Finn! That's amazing.'

She gets it! I am stunned and feel a bit guilty for assuming she wouldn't. Then I hear her calling, 'You lot, come and see! Come and see what Finn's done!'

That's exactly what I wanted to do. Sometimes it happens like that – I know what I want people to do and they do it – and it feels a bit like I can control things, just for a moment. Olivia's thrilled to be the one who shares the news. Sarah appears first, then Mum and Dad.

They gather round and all 'Wow!' over what Finn has done. Dad tells him it's brilliant and the others agree. I see Mum squeeze Dad's hand and they share a smile. Finn continues, apparently oblivious, but I am sure he is pleased.

In this moment I feel full of love for them all: Mum, Dad, Sarah, Finn – and even Olivia. I don't want anything to change.

12

I was on a high after Finn's birthday until the morning when I remembered about the college visit on Wednesday. Sarah's already started packing my bag. We're going to stay overnight – Mum, Sarah and me – in a hotel. I am looking forward to having Mum and Sarah to myself for twenty-four hours, even though I can't get rid of the worry about being sent away.

I'm trying to focus on the professor and the possibility of communication rather than the idea of actually going to Carlstone, so I feel calmer. But as the day goes on, I sense something isn't right. I've got a pain in my back and my lower tummy. I might have an infection. That's happened before and it can get really bad if no one notices.

As Sarah wheels me into the kitchen at dinner time I hear Mum telling Dad that the police have charged the man they were questioning.

'That's good news,' says Sarah. 'Who was it?

Do they know why he did it?'

'Why who did what?' Olivia demands, coming in.

Mum gives Sarah a look as if she shouldn't be asking such things in front of Olivia, which is a bit unfair as Olivia's only just sneaked in and it was Mum who brought it up. I want to know more details too, but Dad changes the subject and starts marvelling about Finn's amazing matchstick squares again. It's so frustrating.

Olivia glowers. Everyone tenses. She's like a lit firework that'll go off with a bang at any moment.

Dad tries to distract her by asking her what she'd like for her birthday. She turns to him, her eyes wide with excitement. It's not her birthday for three months, but this doesn't seem to matter as she takes a deep breath and starts to reel off a very long list. A TV for her room, an iPad, a bigger doll's house. Then Olivia adds, 'That's if I'm still here.'

Mum and Dad look at her in astonishment. 'Of course you'll still be here, love,' says Dad. 'This is your home. You're not going anywhere.'

'I'm not sure I can promise you any of those things for your birthday, though,' Mum adds quickly, catching Dad's eye. 'You'll have to wait and see.'

I suddenly realise that Olivia can rarely have had more than one birthday in one place. It must be hard for her to trust that she's really here to stay.

At least Dad's successfully distracted her from Sarah's question about the murder suspect. I'm still thinking about it, though. Who have the police charged? If it's Dan then Sarah will surely know soon. Or is it someone else altogether?

During the night I kept thinking about it until the pain in my stomach got so bad that I was only thinking about that. Now it's there all the time rather than coming and going. I was willing Sarah to notice this morning, as I can usually rely on her to pick up on it when something's not right. But she seemed distracted.

At school I am uncomfortable all day. Then something happens that stops me thinking about the pain altogether. About an hour after we get home Mum asks where Finn is. No one can find him.

Mum is looking upstairs, Dad downstairs and Sarah the garden. Olivia is 'helping' but clearly getting bored. Dad's searched every cupboard, including the one under the stairs, twice.

Mum comes down. Her hair is all over the place and her eyes panicky. 'He's not here,' she mutters. 'He must have gone outside. He's not here!'

Dad soothes her, stroking her back. 'He's around here somewhere, I'm sure of it. You know how good he is at hiding. He can't open the front door.'

'Maybe he slipped out when someone opened it,' says Mum. She puts her hand to her mouth. 'I went out the back to put some rubbish out. Could he have got out then?'

'He's not in the garden, though,' says Dad, 'and you didn't unlock the gate, did you? He's not tall enough to climb over the gate without standing on something.'

'Finn?' Mum calls. She's trying to sound calm but there's a rough edge to her voice. 'Come on out, love! You're definitely the hide-and-seek winner.'

Mum and Dad are quiet, waiting, listening. There's a sound on the stairs. Mum dashes round the banister . . .

'Oh – Olivia! No sign of Finn?'

'He's probably gone out and walked into the road,' Olivia announces. 'He's got no idea how to cross roads, has he?'

I hear Mum let out a gasp.

'That's enough, Olivia,' says Dad.

'I've been looking for him,' Olivia protests. 'Looking and looking. Just as hard as everyone else – except Jemma.' She's come into view now and gives a glance in my direction.

I am sitting in the lounge, facing out towards the hallway. I have been sitting like this the whole time, facing the cupboard under the stairs – the cupboard where Finn has been hiding for over an hour. I know he's there. I saw him go in. He must be curled up so far into the dark back corner that Dad's two expeditions inside have failed to reveal him.

Dad goes out to walk the streets, though I'm sure he still thinks that Finn is in the house.

'He'll turn up,' Sarah assures Mum.

'You're *sure* nothing happened – nothing that upset him?' Mum asks Sarah.

I look at Sarah's face. Although she helps out with Finn and Olivia her job is caring for me. Mum's not being fair.

'I told you,' Sarah says crossly, 'he seemed fine to me – he was lining up cars in his room.' Sarah looks like she's going to cry. I want to tell her Mum's just worried and doesn't blame her really.

When Dad comes back Mum wants to call the police. Dad wants to wait. They argue. Mum starts really shouting. It's awful. If only I could tell them. If only Finn would come out. I try to make a noise – gurgling noises that turn into, 'Ugghh ugghh.'

Dad then blames Mum for upsetting me. I've just made things worse.

Sarah comes to comfort me. 'Don't worry, Finn will be fine,' she assures me.

In the end Dad phones the police.

I know that Finn must be able to hear this. He knows who the police are, though I'm not sure if he understands enough to realise the worry he's causing.

I wonder why he's hiding. He only does it when he's really stressed out. Once he hid when his teacher was off sick and he didn't like the supply teacher. Perhaps the packing has upset him and he's worried about us being away. That must be it.

Last time he was found after twenty minutes. He was at the back of Mum and Dad's wardrobe, behind the shoe rack.

Dad says the police are on their way. Mum calls

social services too. They have to know he is missing. I feel so sorry for Mum. I'm sure she's worried they'll think she's not looking after us properly.

The doorbell rings.

'That was quick,' says Mum, rushing to answer.

I hear a voice I don't recognise and strain to hear the words. It's not the police – it's the window cleaner wanting to be paid.

'Sorry,' Mum says, sounding frazzled. 'Do you mind coming back? We're having a bit of a crisis. You haven't seen a small boy wandering down the road, have you?'

I don't hear the answer. 'Oh – look, it's not fair on you. I'll grab my purse,' Mum says. She comes into the living room and picks up her bag, without even glancing at me.

'That's funny, I'm sure I had more than that,' she says to herself. 'Ben! Have you got a tenner handy?'

'Sure,' calls Dad. 'Really, couldn't he have waited?'

As Dad goes to the door, Mum looks like she's holding back tears.

When Dad comes back he persuades her to sit down and have a cup of tea while we wait for the police. He pushes me into the kitchen and Mum sits, head in hands, at the table, while Dad puts the kettle on.

Sarah comes in too, followed by a sulky-looking Olivia.

'Let me do that,' Sarah tells Dad, getting some mugs out of the cupboard.

'Can I have a biscuit?' Olivia asks, spying the tin on the shelf above the mugs.

'Please,' Dad reminds her.

Dad pulls down the biscuit tin and opens it. He stares for a moment at the biscuits.

'Can I have one, *pleeeeaaaase*?' Olivia demands.

'I think I'll get the chocolate finger biscuits out,' Dad says loudly.

That's a bit weird. I think the stress has got to him. Olivia gives him a confused look. And then it clicks – he's trying to tempt Finn out. Finger biscuits are Finn's favourite. He always has to have three so that he can line them up.

Dad puts three on Olivia's plate and she beams. 'I'll put three on a plate here for Finn,' Dad says.

'Oh – *Finn*.'

Finn walks into the kitchen and sits down, grabbing all three biscuits tightly. He doesn't meet anyone's eyes, but that's not unusual.

'Where have you been?' Mum demands, as gently as she can manage.

She knows he won't answer, but I see her shoulders relax with relief as she turns to Dad with a smile.

13

The crisis has passed and the house has gone from panic to calm. Soon it is as if nothing happened. Everyone's back doing their own thing and I am back with the pain that has somehow spread while I wasn't thinking about it and is definitely getting worse.

I wish I could focus on something else to put it out of my mind. I try to concentrate on the TV and then Sarah comes in with a basket of washing to fold and I watch her, as she bends and folds at the edge of my vision. My thoughts go back to Dan and the murder. Sarah looks busy but relaxed. It can't be Dan who's been charged. She would have heard something by now, wouldn't she? But just because they've charged someone, that doesn't mean they've definitely got the right man, does it?

A programme comes on about people who are training for the next Paralympics. There's a woman with cerebral palsy who is hoping to compete in archery and even though I'll never do anything like that, it is inspiring to watch her. She's spent hours and hours each week practising to get this good and she looks so determined.

Still it's difficult to concentrate. The pain won't go away. I try thinking about Jodi instead – about her letter and how brilliant it would be to get another one. But nothing's come. I hope she hasn't changed her mind . . .

I'd love so much to be able to communicate with her. The professor guy who's coming to Carlstone – could he have the answer for me? Even though the college thing is scary, the idea that I might be able to communicate is so huge that most of the time I don't let myself think about it. All through my life people have tried different things – from pointing at letter boards to eye-gaze technology – but nothing worked. I remember when I was ten we all got excited because a new teacher taught me to say yes and no by blinking. But then I got really ill with an infection. I was in hospital for ages and when I felt better I couldn't control my blinking any more.

Is there really a chance? I have so much I want to say – but I'm scared to hope. What if by the time

I met my sister I could actually do it? When Sarah goes on about Dan I could interrupt her and tell her exactly what he's really like. When Finn hides, I could tell them where he is or tempt him out myself with biscuits. And right now I could say that I'm in pain and where it hurts.

I know even if there is a way, it won't be easy. I found it hard enough with the blinking. It was a lot of effort to control it. And all the questions made me feel panicky. I was used to watching, not deciding, and if I didn't respond quickly people either kept repeating the question over and over, which was infuriating, or just gave up, which was even worse. And of course nobody ever asked me the questions I wanted them to ask.

Sometimes I blinked by accident and gave an answer I didn't intend – I blinked 'no' when Mum asked if I'd like ketchup and ever since, for the last four years, she's stopped giving it to me. I don't like it on everything, but I really do like it on chips.

At least when I could blink I was able to show how much I knew and understood. They were amazed to see that I could read. I had an American teacher at school when I was six, Miss Moray, who taught us all as if we were as bright as any other six year olds. She went through all the letters and basic words. She said that's what they do in the US. My next teacher didn't bother with reading at all, but I've always read signs and labels, and Mum often put the subtitles on the TV too. What I found hard was making choices. Mum said she'd always known how bright I was, but I think she was the only one. Even Dad had never seemed sure although he'd tried hard not to show it.

After I couldn't control the blinking, it's hard to admit, but part of me felt relieved. It was a relief to go back to just watching and not having to decide. But it's different now. I'd give anything for the chance to be able to do it again. I'm older and there's so much I want to say. I want to talk to Jodi. I want to make my own choices. 'Yes' and 'no' won't be enough, though – not to tell them about Dan.

This woman I'm watching has been training so hard and she's studying at university too. Her disability is much milder than mine, but it is still impressive to watch. And she's putting in all that effort with no certainty that she'll even make it into the Paralympic team. It's all about daring to hope, isn't it? You have to dare to think you might win. If I dare to think I might communicate again, it might come true.

But it also might not. And the disappointment would be a million times harder.

The pain in my back is getting worse – a constant dull throb.

Sarah's phone rings. It's Richard. Sarah is still upset thinking Mum blames her for Finn going missing. She's telling Richard about it. 'No, no,' she says – and I think he might have suggested coming over. 'I've no time off until the weekend,' she tells him. 'I'll be fine – it helps to talk to you. You've made me feel much better.'

She's no sooner put down her phone than it rings again. She answers without even looking at the screen.

'R– Dan, hi!' She doesn't tell him about Finn.

'What, *now*?' she says. 'I can't – I've got to put Jemma to bed soon. And to be honest, I'm worn out. I've had such a crap day . . .'

I wonder what he's saying. 'No, no, you can't,' Sarah tells him.

Dan's not like Richard, though – he won't take no for an answer.

Sarah puts her phone down and sighs. 'He's coming

over,' she tells me. 'It's not that I don't want to see him, it's just that I'm so tired.'

So now I know for sure – the police haven't got Dan. It must be someone else.

Mum comes downstairs and Sarah explains to her that Dan is popping in. Mum is clearly not happy from the abrupt tone of her voice.

'He won't be here long, I promise,' says Sarah. 'I tried to tell him not to, but he insisted.'

'What a day,' Mum says, sighing. 'I feel like I'm going mad. Oh, Sarah – you didn't borrow money from my purse, did you?'

'What? No, I didn't. Why would I have done that?' Sarah demands.

'I know you buy things for Jemma sometimes and I thought you might –'

'I wouldn't without asking!' Sarah retorts.

'Forget I said anything,' Mum says sheepishly. 'I probably spent it without realising.'

Sarah is silent. I feel so powerless. The tension between them hurts me inside and frightens me, but there's nothing I can do. If Sarah's not happy here, if she stops getting on with Mum, then she won't want to stay.

Dan arrives half an hour later. I am still up and in the lounge. Mum and Dad are upstairs. I have a partial view into the hall and I am shocked to see him grab Sarah as she opens the door. For a moment I think he's going to hurt her, but he pulls her towards him and kisses her hard. Sarah moves back, laughing awkwardly.

'What's up, babe?' he asks, flinching as if reeling from her rejection.

'Nothing's up,' Sarah tells him. She's speaking quietly – but not too quietly for me to hear. 'I've told you – you can't keep turning up like this. You know what Lorraine –'

'And I've told you, I can't keep away, babe!' says Dan. 'Have you thought about what I said?'

'You know how I feel about you,' Sarah says softly. 'But I have to be here overnight for Jemma – I can't live at yours.'

'Give up the job! I'll take care of you.' It's Dan who's speaking quietly now.

My heart lurches. She won't do that, will she?

I listen hard to hear her reply. She starts with a kiss, which doesn't feel like a good sign. I wish Mum hadn't given her such a hard time. She's feeling fed up here and now Dan's offering her a way out. But what about me?

'I want to be with you, but Jemma needs me,' Sarah tells him, and I heave a sigh of relief which comes out as a slight snort. Dan turns towards the lounge doorway and meets my eyes briefly with a look of disgust.

'They'll get someone else no problem,' he says, turning back to Sarah. 'There's loads of people after carer jobs.'

'I like my job,' Sarah argues.

'Do you, though? Really?' Dan's shaking his head. 'You've got the patience of a saint, babe, but no one does this kind of job unless they have to.'

I feel my muscles tighten.

Sarah pauses. 'I . . . Look, let's talk about it properly next time I see you.'

'I'll take you out, then. When're you free?' Dan demands.

'Hang on, I'll check,' Sarah tells him.

She's gone to check her days on the calendar and my worst fear comes true. Dan comes into the living room. He stands close – bends over me – staring at me, screwing up his nose. Then he shakes his head.

'You think she's gonna stay here, don't you? But you just wait –'

At that moment his mobile rings and he moves away as he answers it. I can breathe again though I'm horrified by the way he spoke to me.

'Hiya, Billy! What's up, mate?' he says. His voice is quiet but brash, different from the cheerful, friendly one he uses with Sarah, and not that nasty voice he uses for me.

'Yeah! It's sorted? Behind the Co-op, is it? I know where you mean . . . Sure thing. See ya.'

He puts the phone in his pocket just as Sarah comes back.

'I've got next Thursday off,' she tells him.

'That's over a week away! You can stay over then, though, right?'

She nods, and then gives him a nudge towards the door, telling him he has to go now. He jokes that she's always trying to get rid of him and Sarah rolls her eyes and points upstairs, like it's because of Mum. Then Dan whispers something in Sarah's ear and gives her another kiss.

I'm so relieved when he's gone.

*

'He loves me, Jemma,' Sarah says dreamily, a little later, as she carefully brushes my teeth. She's supporting my head with her other hand in case I suddenly jolt. 'And I love him too.'

I feel sick. I wish I could tell her he's a vile creep.

'Big day tomorrow,' she says, changing the subject. 'Bet you're excited!'

I'd almost forgotten about the college visit. I wonder what the professor will say. Is there really a chance . . .?

14

'Have you seen Jemma's red fleece?' Sarah calls to Mum.

It's chaos this morning as Sarah runs round finding last-minute things to put in my case. I seem to need an awful lot of stuff for one night's stay. Mum is trying to finish her own packing and Dad is attempting to single-handedly get Olivia and Finn ready for school.

My back and tummy pain are even worse and I have this kind of fuzzy, giddy feeling. It's definitely an infection. Sarah thinks it's just anxiety about the day ahead. Typical. When I was anxious before they thought it was physical and now it's the other way round.

'Here it is,' says Mum, handing my fleece to Sarah.

Mum turns to me and looks concerned. 'There's no need for you to be worried about today – I promise.'

The pain in my back has developed into a throb and it is spreading outwards, surging through me. I feel hot – too hot.

Someone's speaking. Sarah's moving closer.

I think she says, 'Something's not right,' but the words sound blurry. Her face, close to mine, is blurry too. Everything is spinning.

I am vaguely aware of being lifted out of my wheelchair, faces bending over me, voices talking. Then the jolting movement of the ambulance, the trolley, the white curtains swishing, bright lights, the drip, the monitor. These are all familiar to me. I've spent a lot of time at this hospital.

Mum is sitting by my bed now, holding my hand. Her hand is warm and safe. I drift off and wake to find the hand holding mine is larger, firmer. Mum has been replaced by Dad. Later it is a smaller, long-fingered hand, as Sarah chats away to me.

Mum jokes about the convenience of living only a ten-minute drive from the hospital. It wasn't something she or Dad thought about when they bought the house years ago but it has proved very useful.

Mum, Dad and Sarah do a rota. There is always someone by my side. I am so glad they are there. I would completely panic otherwise. Some nurses do stuff without even bothering to talk to me, as if there's no point explaining anything. Whoever's with me will ask and make sure I know what's going to happen, but I'd be terrified if some stranger just lifted my arm and started putting a needle in me or something.

Sarah squeezes my hand. She seems agitated. I can feel her pulse faster than it should be.

'You awake, Jem?' she says, seeing my eyes open. 'How're you feeling? The pain should be better after all the stuff they're pumping into you.'

She gives a nod towards the drip and smiles.

She's right. The pain is better, though I feel very weak and my head feels heavy and peculiar.

'I'm so sorry I didn't realise how bad it was, Jemma,' she tells me, giving my hand another squeeze. 'Your mum blames me for not spotting it earlier. I feel awful.'

Sarah thinks Mum blamed her for Finn going missing and now for this. I wish Mum would stop having a go at her.

It's only the next day, when my head is a bit clearer, that it sinks in that I missed the trip to the college. I'm not going to meet the professor.

Mum seems to realise what I'm thinking.

'Don't worry, love, we'll rearrange the trip.

I actually spoke to Professor Spalding and he said he'd be very interested to meet you.'

She isn't saying, 'And he's sure he can help.'

But at least there is still a chance.

I'm dozing, aware that Sarah is holding my hand. She's been here for a long time. When I manage to open my eyes briefly I see that hers are half closing. Then suddenly there's a voice. Someone else is in the room.

'Hi, babe,' he says.

My stomach clenches.

Sarah sits up and turns round.

'What are you doing here?' she asks. It's something she seems to say to Dan a lot.

'I was worried about you – sitting here for hours on end. And I was right to worry, eh? Look at you. You're knackered.'

'I'm OK,' Sarah says.

'Yeah, sure,' he says, raising his eyebrows in disbelief. 'Come on, let me take you for a coffee.'

'But I can't leave Jemma,' Sarah says, sounding shocked that he would suggest it.

'She'll be all right,' says Dan. 'It's not like she can run off or anything.'

'Dan!' Sarah exclaims.

'Tell you what, I'll stay with Jemma while you get a coffee,' says Dan. 'That way she won't be on her own and you get a break. Win, win.'

'I shouldn't . . . but . . . oh, babe, would you really do that?' Sarah asks. He leans forwards and kisses her.

If there is any time that I'd most want Sarah's mind-reading skills to kick in, this would be it. With every thought, I urge her to stay. I want her to see it in my eyes. But she's not even looking at me.

'If you're worried at all, press that bell,' Sarah tells him. 'I'm sure she'll be fine, though.'

She turns to me, stroking my arm. I stare at her – hoping she will see the distress on my face. I even try to make a sound, but just a horrid 'erhhhhh' comes out.

'I'll be back in five minutes, I promise,' she assures me.

Then she's gone.

15

Dan doesn't sit down beside my bed and hold my hand – which is a relief. Instead he paces round the bed slowly. I begin to wish he would sit down. I am happier when I can see him than when I can't and when he's on the other side of the bed I can't see him at all. Now he's back on this side.

Is he really here because he can't bear to be apart from Sarah . . . or is he checking up on her?

He fixes me with a sarcastic smile. 'Always causing trouble, aren't you, Jemma? It would be much easier if they just kept you here. Or . . .'

He's moved back from the bed now and he seems to be looking closely at everything – the tube going into me from the drip with antibiotics, the plugs in the wall.

I can see what he's doing. He's trying to wind me up again – pretending to look for a way to switch me off! At least, I hope he's pretending . . .

No! He's crouching down by the wall. He's actually doing it! I want Sarah. I need Sarah. A gurgling noise comes from deep in my throat. Dan stands up, holding a plug in his hand, laughing. 'What's that? Is that the best you can do for a scream?'

Then I realise – the lamp beside my bed has gone off. He's pulled out the plug! I shouldn't have panicked. Of course, I'm not on a life support machine. I was just so scared of him . . . I know he wants me out of the way. He wants Sarah to himself.

He pushes the plug back and chuckles as the light flickers on.

I *wish* Sarah would come back. It must have been five minutes by now.

He comes nearer, sits down on the chair by my bed. I listen to his heavy breathing. I wait – unsure what he's going to do next. He's still looking around. I can see his eyes on the box of disposable gloves. Now he's looking behind me. Does he have his eye on my pillow? Am I imagining it – or is he still thinking of ways . . .?

'All OK?'

Sarah's voice is such a welcome relief I feel myself

sink back against the softness of the bed. The thudding in my chest slows down.

'Yeah, Jemma's been just fine,' Dan assures her.

'It was so sweet of you to do this,' Sarah says, kissing him.

'Any time,' Dan tells her, 'no prob.' He kisses her back.

Dan leaves, giving me a parting smile that makes my heart shudder. Sarah sits down and soon a nurse comes in to check my pulse, temperature and blood pressure.

She tuts. 'Pulse is higher than it should be,' she comments. 'I'll get a doctor to check her.'

'Dan got your pulse up?' Sarah teases. 'You don't fancy him, do you? He's all mine, Jemma!'

If only I could tell her . . .

Mum arrives at that moment and is concerned to hear about my pulse, fussing over me.

'Did you notice anything?' Mum asks Sarah. 'Has she been awake or asleep?'

Sarah scowls. Mum is being a bit aggressive with the questions. Luckily she is saved from answering by the doctor. He takes my pulse again and it's already going back to normal. My temperature and blood pressure are fine.

'Nothing to worry about,' he says, smiling at Mum and then at me.

Sarah leaves without saying goodbye to Mum.

There's a strange feeling when I am finally home. It's hard to explain, but it's like things have shifted while I've been away, even though it was only a couple of days. One of the chairs in the lounge has been moved round and there's a small spiky plant in a pot on the hall shelf. It wasn't there before. There's always been a china elephant on that shelf and nothing else, but he's been pushed along and the spiky plant is in the middle. Am I getting as bad as Finn – not liking any change?

The second, far more important thing is that Sarah isn't here. Mum gave her extra time off because she'd spent so much time at the hospital with me. Sarah's gone to stay with Dan – like he wanted.

I want her here and I'm worried about her being alone with *him*; she has no idea what he's really like. What if she lets something slip about going to the concert with Richard? What if Dan already knows that something is going on?

Finn comes in and I hope for some sign that

he's pleased I'm back. Maybe I should know better – but I've always felt we understand each other. I can hear him moving about behind me, but he doesn't let me see him. Then I hear a sound I've heard before.

Bang, bang, bang.

He is banging his head against the wall – rhythmically, over and over.

'Stop, Finn!' I want to yell. Finn used to do this a lot. But the last two years he's done it much less. I think me being away and the change to his routine may have really upset him. Perhaps that's why he's staying there, behind me. He wants me to know he's angry. I feel so bad. I don't want to upset Finn.

'Oh, Finn! There's no need for that,' says Mum, coming into the lounge. 'Let's find something for you to play with.'

My muscles relax as Mum takes the matchsticks out of the cupboard and Finn starts lining them up.

'Look what's come today!' Mum is waving an envelope at me.

I get a gush of happiness as I watch her open it. A letter! A letter from Jodi.

'*Dear Jemma*,' Mum reads.

'*I was so excited when your mum wrote and said she had read my letter to you. I hope you were as pleased as I was to find out you have a sister!*

'*She says she really hopes to find a way for you to communicate so you can write back or even talk to me one day. That would be so cool. I looked online and I found stuff about head pointers and eye-gaze technology – it all sounds so clever! I've been reading up about cerebral palsy too. I really want to understand what it's like.*

'*I've printed out a photo of Fluff, this time. I hope your mum will send me one of you.*

'*I hope we will be able to meet one day soon!*

'*Love, Jodi x x x.*'

'She sounds lovely, doesn't she, Jemma?' Mum says, sighing. 'I know she's keen to meet you and I'm sure you'd like to meet her too, but I still think it's best to take things slowly. I'd like to see Professor Spalding first.'

Finn has stopped lining up sticks and is sitting, rocking.

I understand what Mum's saying. It would be

amazing to be able to 'talk' to Jodi somehow. Even just with a 'yes' and 'no'. But I don't know how long I'd have to wait. I want to meet Jodi now.

16

When Dan drops Sarah off the next day Mum thanks him for the plant he bought. No wonder I didn't like it.

'You're looking so much better, Jem,' Sarah tells me, smiling warmly. We're in the bathroom and Sarah has just emptied my bag. 'You gave me a scare, you really did.'

I gave myself a scare too. But right now I'm more interested in whether Sarah had her talk with Dan about moving in.

'Your mum was telling me that the professor guy is going to be back at Carlstone College next Thursday,' Sarah continues, 'just for a day. After that he's off to the US for three months. I think we should go for it if you're feeling well enough.'

I'm still feeling tired after my infection, but I do want to meet him. Even if there's only a small chance of anything changing. Now Mum's fixed on me meeting him before she'll let me meet Jodi, I have an even greater incentive than before. But if he can't help me, will I still get to meet her?

Sarah is pushing me towards the kitchen for dinner when she stops and I jolt in the chair. Her phone is ringing upstairs.

'I'll just get it – it might be Dan. I won't be a sec.'

She leaves me outside the kitchen. Mum's not in there, but I can see Olivia through the doorway. She's on a stool by the kitchen counter. What is she up to? She climbs on to the counter top and opens a high cupboard, the one where Mum keeps the sweets. She has a bag of Haribos in her hand as she jumps down and I see her stash them in the pocket of her jeans.

Sarah's back. 'It was Richard,' she whispers, 'about the concert. I can't wait!'

I'm glad she's confiding in me again. It feels more normal. For a moment I imagine that I'm going with Sarah instead of Richard. I'd definitely be just as excited as she is. I've seen concerts on TV and I think it would be amazing to hear a band live, especially Glowlight.

It is macaroni cheese for dinner. I like pasta, but cheese sauce sometimes gets stuck in my throat and makes me cough. Sarah is feeding me. Finn's not eating but is rocking backwards and forwards in his chair. He's not so keen on pasta either – maybe because it is so curvy – especially macaroni. Olivia has wolfed hers down.

She looks at Sarah. 'Do you like staying all night with Dan?' she giggles.

'Yeah, I had a great time, thanks,' Sarah tells her.

'Did you have sex?'

I cough up some cheese sauce.

'Olivia!' Dad splutters. 'You don't ask people questions like that.'

'I was only interested.' Olivia's mouth turns sulky.

I stop coughing. Sarah wipes my mouth with some kitchen towel and gives me a drink. Her cheeks are pink.

'How was school?' Dad asks Olivia.

'Melissa's not my friend any more,' Olivia tells him.

'I didn't know you had a friend called Melissa,' Mum comments.

'She was only my friend for one day and now she's not,' says Olivia.

'Why's that?' asks Dad.

'I don't wanna talk about it.' Olivia folds her arms.

Dad turns his attention to trying to coax Finn to eat. He has a few mouthfuls.

'I think we should take Jemma to meet that guy,' Sarah tells Mum. 'She seems to have made a good recovery, haven't you, Jemma?'

'That's great,' says Mum and she actually gives Sarah what looks like a genuine smile. 'I think so too.'

I'm relieved that the decision is made and even more relieved to see Mum and Sarah talking normally to each other. Olivia and Finn go off to play while Sarah finishes feeding me and Dad turns on the radio for the news.

I'm not really listening until I catch the name Ryan Blake. Dad turns it up and shushes everyone.

'Jay Wiggins, who was charged last week with the murder of Ryan Blake, has been released after a witness came forward corroborating his alibi. The twenty-five-year-old car mechanic had been in custody for a week. He described his relief that his name has been cleared, saying that the whole experience had been a "complete nightmare".'

Sarah's phone, now in her pocket, rings even before the news item has finished.

'Sorry,' she says, taking it out and looking as if she is switching it off.

'Jay Wiggins?' says Dad. 'Is he someone Paula knew about? Did she ever mention him?'

'Not that I can recall,' says Mum.

'Well, looks like the police got it wrong. Hopefully he's not the only suspect they identified.'

Maybe they do have another suspect. Maybe it's Dan. Sarah says nothing about it, of course, as she gets me ready for bed. She starts reading me a vampire romance book. I like it and it makes a change from Agatha Christie.

Her phone keeps buzzing as she reads. I get a glimpse of the screen one time it does as she picks it up. I see Dan's name. It's there and then it fades away again.

17

I doze on and off for most of the journey to Carlstone College – Mum's decided we will do it in a day, so we leave really early. Any time I open my eyes, Sarah is either texting or looking at her phone. When I wake up again, I'm refreshed, if a bit stiff. We've arrived.

Mum lowers the ramp and Sarah detaches the wheelchair from its clamps and wheels me down.

'Thank God the traffic was good,' Mum comments.

'And the sun's come out for us too,' adds Sarah.

I share their optimisim as I am turned to face the college building. It is modern and bigger than I expected. I'd had an image in my mind from a film set in an old boarding school. This is nothing like that.

The glass doors open automatically as we approach and we are welcomed by the smiling face of the woman at the reception desk. She tells us to take a seat and wait.

Sarah wheels me into a space beside some seats, and she and Mum sit down.

Opposite me I can see a certificate on the wall that says *Carlstone College, Centre of Excellence for Augmentative and Alternative Communication*. I've heard Mum talking about AAC and I knew it was to do with communication systems for people who can't speak, but I never knew what it stood for until now. I don't know what 'augmentative' means, though.

Students pass us – some in wheelchairs, some being pushed, some pushing themselves and others walking. They all look much older than me. I wonder what it would be like to be a student here. I have to admit I get a tingle of excitement at the thought before the fear and worries about everything it would mean take over. I won't think about all that now. Instead I distract myself by wondering what the professor will look like. I don't have to wait long to find out.

A tall man with thick curly hair comes striding towards us.

'You must be Jemma,' he says, crouching to make eye contact. 'I'm very pleased to meet you.' He attempts to shake my stiff, curled hand. He has kind eyes and he is looking deeply into mine. I feel slightly afraid. My eyes give nothing away – I know that.

He turns to greet Mum and Sarah. I'm glad he spoke to me first.

'Follow me,' he tells us.

We follow him down a wide corridor. There are ramps everywhere and the ride is smooth. The big windows throw squares of brightness on to the clean red floor.

We stop at a door, which Professor Spalding opens and holds for us as we all go in.

The room is like a doctor's office, with desk, computer and chairs. There is a spiky plant on the windowsill. I hope that isn't a bad omen.

'I very much hope I can help you, Jemma,' he tells me. 'As you know, new communication systems are being developed all the time.'

'Yes,' says Mum. 'We've tried various kinds of AAC with Jemma and also with our son who has severe autism. We've not had much luck, to be honest, with either of them.'

Professor Spalding nods. 'But you believe Jemma understands cause and effect?'

'Definitely,' says Mum. 'She was able to communicate "yes" and "no" by blinking when she was ten. She was taught to read and we know that she understands a huge amount. We're sure she laughs sometimes too.' Mum goes on to explain about my illness. Then she adds, 'I know some of these communication systems can be expensive, but Jemma does have some funds from a medical negligence case. The money pays for her to have her own carer. It's not a bottomless pit, though.'

'Hmmm,' says Professor Spalding, tapping his pencil on the table. 'We can worry about funding later. I'd like to do a few tests that will help me assess the best means of communication for you, Jemma. You must understand that even if we find a way, it will take some time to master. Babies learn to speak by making sounds, babbling and then gradually learning to express words. Even though your understanding may be good, it will not be easy for you to put phrases together, select words, etc. You will have to be patient.'

Patience is something I know plenty about – though I am feeling impatient now. I wish he'd stop talking and get on with it.

He tries to get me to look left and right. The first time he asks I am able to do it. He looks so pleased.

But when he asks me to repeat it I can't. I try. I try so hard. I see the pleasure turn to disappointment as the light in his eyes fades.

He tries to see if I can move anything else – tilt my head, lift a finger, clench a cheek, open and close my mouth. My body sometimes moves. My head jolts. I automatically close my mouth to swallow food, but I cannot do it voluntarily. He asks me to make sounds too, but I can't – not intentionally.

He even tells a bad joke about a chicken, but it isn't funny enough to make me laugh. I can only laugh spontaneously, I can't make it happen.

He soon realises what I already know.

I have no control.

18

'What makes you so certain that Jemma's brain is unaffected by her illness?' the professor asks Mum and Sarah.

I can't see their faces – but I know they both believe in me.

'It's an instinct,' says Mum. 'We both feel it.'

'Yes,' Sarah agrees.

'My husband too,' says Mum. 'And the doctors said at the time there was no reason why it should have been affected.'

Professor Spalding touches his lip and looks at me thoughtfully.

What is he thinking? Does he think I'm brain-dead?

'Can you sniff for me, Jemma?' he asks.

Sniff? I think *he's* mad now.

'Breathe in through your nose – as hard as you can,' he tells me.

For a moment I panic – I can't think how. It's not

something I've ever thought about before. It's also so rare that anyone actually asks me to *do* anything. Then I calm myself. I have to hurry or he might give up.

I sniff.

'Now breathe out through your nose.'

I can do that too – though I'd love to know where he's going with this.

'Now again,' he says.

I breathe in and out through my nose. I am pleased to be able to actually respond, but also confused. Everybody knows that I can breathe.

'Hmmm,' says Professor Spalding. 'Interesting.'

He pauses.

'I don't think the eye movements are going to be useful,' he tells me, turning to Mum and Sarah too. 'They are not consistent enough. However, a colleague of mine is developing a new communication tool, based on sniffing. It's hard to tell if Jemma would have enough control, but it might be worth a try.'

'Communicate with sniffing?' Sarah repeats. 'I've never heard of that!'

I sniff again, just to make sure they know I can do it.

Professor Spalding continues. 'My colleague Alon Katz and his team are based in Israel. When he's next in the UK perhaps he could meet you and see if it might be suitable. We hope he'll be over in a few months.'

A few months! That's so long!

Could I really use sniffing to communicate, though? Would I be able to say the things I want and need to say? I think about Dan. Can you sniff that someone is a murderer?

19

After lunch Catherine, the deputy head of the college, shows us round. She has beautiful shiny dark hair and a warm smile, and she is so bubbly and jokey with the students that I sense she loves working here.

'We have students using all kinds of AAC devices,' she tells us. She introduces us to some of the students. One girl, who is only able to raise one eyebrow, proudly shows us that she can select words on a computer and move between screens for different categories of words. She raises her eyebrow repeatedly until the pointer reaches the word she wants on the screen and then she stops. After a second, the word appears on the line below. Then she carries on. It's very slow, but eventually she types, I GO MUSIC, and a voice speaks her words.

'Don't let us hold you up, Kaya!' says Catherine. Then she adds, 'Kaya's a total music geek.'

I feel a gut-wrenching pull. How amazing it would

be to spell out words on a screen like that. Would I be able to do it – by sniffing? Is it possible? We see the bedrooms and bathrooms, which are bright and spacious. Two students share each room so I realise I'd have a room-mate if I came here.

Mum says, 'I think this would be a fantastic place for you in a few years' time. What do you think, Jemma?'

Sarah smiles at me too.

Catherine and Mum start discussing funding applications, but I am thinking about what she said. *A few years' time!* They weren't planning to send me here sooner. I was worrying for no reason.

On the journey home I start to feel giddy. Sarah notices I am flushed and gets Mum to pull over. My temperature is up. She gives me medicine. We have to stop three times. I feel every jolt and jerk of the car. Then we are stuck in traffic.

'She doesn't look well,' Mum moans. 'This was a mistake.'

'We didn't know the traffic would be like this,' says Sarah. 'It's just bad luck.'

'I wasn't sure,' says Mum. 'I thought it might be too soon – but you convinced me.'

'You said you felt the same!' Sarah protests, her voice getting louder and higher. 'We both wanted to do it. Stop blaming me for stuff!'

'Calm down,' says Mum, even though her voice is just as agitated. 'I wasn't . . . Look, we both want the best for Jemma. Let's not row about it.'

Sarah is silent. My skin feels prickly. I feel like crying when they argue.

At last the traffic clears and we are moving, though the horrible atmosphere in the car isn't going anywhere. But I feel worse – hot and sick. My clothes are sticking to me.

When we finally get home we are greeted by Dad. He looks washed out. He frowns with concern when he sees how flushed I am. He's so pale. And I'm only adding to his worries.

Sarah puts me to bed although the clock on the wall says it's only 6 p.m.

'I'm sure you'll feel better after a good rest, Jem,' she tells me. 'I'll keep a close eye on you. We don't want another stint in that hospital, do we?'

No, we certainly don't. The image of Dan holding up the plug he'd pulled out flashes through my head.

'I'm sorry if today was too much,' she says, gently

bathing my hot forehead with a cool flannel. 'I'm sure you'll be fine after a good night's sleep. The college was great, wasn't it?'

It is a relief to be surrounded by the softness of my bed after the jolting of the wheelchair in the car. I feel better already. My eyes close, but I don't want to sleep. I want Sarah to stay with me. I feel safe with her here and while she's with me I also know she's safe from Dan. It's not much, but it's the only way I can protect her. But my eyes are closing and I hear her footsteps on the stairs.

She's left my door open and bits of conversation drift my way from the kitchen. Mum is telling Dad about the day. It takes a while. Then Mum says, 'Everything all right here?'

'Not really,' I hear Dad say. I strain to listen.

'I dropped them at school and went to work,' Dad tells Mum, 'and then I got a call to say Olivia had attacked a boy and I'd have to come and get her. She must have hit him hard – he's lost a tooth.'

'*What?*' Mum exclaims. 'Have you talked to her about it? Did she tell you what happened?'

'She said it wasn't her fault. I asked if he hit her first and she said, "No – you just don't get it," and she wouldn't talk to me after that. She's been sulking in her room most of the day. They've excluded her until Monday.'

I hear breathing close by and my eyes open. I assume it's Sarah, back to check on me, but it's Olivia I see standing in my doorway. The light in the hall behind her means she is mostly in shadow, but I can see that she is looking towards the kitchen, listening intently to Mum and Dad like I am. I can only see the side of her face, but her eye is glistening; she's close to tears.

She looks like such a sad little girl I feel sorry for her for a moment. It's hard to believe she hit a boy so hard his tooth came out.

She turns and sees me in bed and her eyebrows go up.

'Are you ill?' She reaches over and touches my forehead, like she's seen Mum and Sarah do. 'Yeah, you're a bit hot.'

She sits silently for a couple of minutes, biting skin from around her fingernails.

'There's no point in telling anyone what really happened cos no one believes anything I say,' she says finally.

I want to tell her that they will believe her. Even if her teachers don't, Mum and Dad will. I'll believe her. Is she going to tell *me*? I look at her, hoping so much that she will.

'Dylan found out I'm in care and he's told everyone. He keeps being mean about it, like saying I'm in care cos my real mum hates me. He winds me up till I can't take it any more. It's so unfair. I didn't mean to hit him that hard. Blood was coming out of his mouth and everything! It was disgusting. But he shouldn't be mean all the time. It's not fair that I'm sent home and he just gets away with it.'

Poor Olivia. She shouldn't have hit him, but Dylan does sound really nasty. She should have told someone when it happened instead of lashing out – but even now, if she explained, at least people would be more understanding.

'She's not upstairs!' I hear Mum calling anxiously.

'She was,' Dad says, also sounding worried. 'Olivia? Olivia!'

Olivia doesn't move for a moment, but then she calls out, 'I'm in here.'

'She's in Jemma's room,' Dad calls to Mum.

'Thank goodness,' I hear Mum say. 'What are

you doing in there? Jemma's trying to sleep – she's not well. Come here, Olivia. Tell me what's been going on.'

As Olivia leaves my room she bursts into tears.

20

I wake up in the morning, instantly aware that I don't feel feverish. I feel pleasantly cool – it is such a relief.

Dad comes in. I've been turned to face the window. He draws the curtains and I am pleased to see that the colour has returned to his face – a nice rosy pinkness.

'Sounds like you had quite a day yesterday,' he says. He eases me into a sitting position with his firm, careful hands and cradles me to keep me upright, his arm round my shoulder, comfortingly.

'Sounds like you did too,' I want to say.

Sarah comes in and Dad explains that she'll have two at home today as I'm not well and Olivia is suspended.

'Maybe Olivia could read to Jemma,' he says.

'Do you want to talk about what happened with Dylan?' Sarah asks Olivia, as we sit in the lounge, later. 'Your mum says you haven't told her anything.'

'No, thanks,' says Olivia.

'Why don't you read to Jemma?' Sarah suggests half-heartedly. She's been trying, and failing, to keep Olivia occupied all morning.

'No, can I watch something?' says Olivia. 'I'm sure Jemma wants to watch something too.'

'Being excluded is meant to be a punishment – not a chance to watch TV all day,' Sarah tells her. 'Really I should get you scrubbing the floors or set you some sums to do.'

'No, please – not that!' Olivia has a look of horror on her face and Sarah grins.

So she reads to me – her school reading book that is about a pony with magic powers. She holds it so I can see the words. I can read, but my eyes flicker a lot so it is hard to look at a page of text. My eyes get tired quickly too. Olivia struggles a bit with reading and I doubt she is as good as most nine-year-olds. The book seems babyish for her.

'Lovely, Olivia!' Sarah tells her when she's finished two tedious chapters. 'If you had a magic pony like that, what would you do?'

'I'd ride round the world on him and get him to

kick all the bad people with his super hooves – kick them until they're dead!'

I snort. Sarah's eyes widen and I can see she's trying not to laugh as well. 'Oh, Olivia! How would you know who the bad people were?'

'I just would,' Olivia says, closing the book with a *snap*.

Sarah's phone beeps.

'Is that Dan?' Olivia asks, cheekily trying to see over Sarah's shoulder as she pulls out the phone.

'Don't be so nosy!' Sarah gives her a nudge.

'Who is it, then?'

Sarah sighs. 'Actually, it's about a gig I'm going to tomorrow night. Have you heard of Glowlight?'

'You're going to see a band?' Olivia says. 'Cool – can I come too?'

'No, it's not for kids,' says Sarah. 'I'll play you some of their songs if you like.'

'Yeah!' Olivia jumps up, chucking the book on to the sofa.

Sarah finds a song and the intro starts playing out of her phone.

I sing the words to myself inside my head as Sarah and Olivia bop around the living room. I love

Glowlight and wish Sarah would play the music more often.

Mum comes in while we're having lunch. She plonks the post down on the kitchen table and looks briefly through the pile.

'Two for you, Jemma. You're popular today!'

'Why aren't there any for me?' Olivia demands. 'No one ever writes to me.'

'Most of the post that comes is very boring, Olivia,' Mum points out. 'Jemma's letters are mainly hospital appointments. This looks like one here.' She tears it open. 'Ah, it's from Professor Spalding.'

I wait impatiently while Mum reads the letter and I try to read her expression.

'Good news and bad news, Jemma,' Mum says. 'Mr Katz, the guy from Israel, would like to meet you when he's here for a conference – but it's not until July.'

July is five months away! It feels like forever.

'I'll read you the other letter later,' she says, tapping it gently.

My head buzzes. That must mean it's from Jodi, but Mum doesn't want to read it in front of the others.

I can't wait to hear what she says. But Mum said

we should wait to see if I can communicate before we meet. Is she really going to make me wait five months? And then whatever they have planned may not even work anyway . . .

'So what have you been up to?' Mum asks Olivia, as she makes herself a sandwich.

'Sarah put on her music and we've been dancing for hours,' Olivia tells Mum.

Mum frowns at Sarah and then turns to Olivia. 'I'm not sure you should be having so much fun when you've been excluded,' she tells her.

'She did read to Jemma,' Sarah says defensively, 'and Jemma enjoyed watching her dance.'

Every time I think Sarah and Mum are getting on better they start snapping at each other again.

'I've been to your school this morning,' Mum tells Olivia. 'Your teacher has given me some work for you to do, so that should keep you busy this afternoon.'

'Bo-ring!' groans Olivia.

When lunch is over, Mum leaves Sarah to help Olivia with her schoolwork and pushes my wheelchair into the lounge. She sits close to me on the sofa and reads me my letter from Jodi.

Jodi sounds so chatty and lovely. She tells me

how she went out for pizza with her boyfriend and he knocked his drink over and it went all over the pizza so it was a soggy mess! And how her team won their last three hockey matches and might win the championship. She says Mum sent a photo of me and she can see our hair is the same colour. Again, she is asking to meet me.

'Jemma,' Mum sighs, looking up at me. 'I really thought it would be better to wait for you to meet Mr Katz and try his communication system before you met Jodi. But that means such a long wait for both of you. I'll talk to your dad, see what he thinks.'

My heart is racing. I'm sure Dad will agree. I'm sure both of them know how much this means to me.

All night, I can't stop thinking about Jodi. Over breakfast I try to suss out if Mum has spoken to Dad yet. And then, when the others have left the room, she finally says, 'Jemma, I've chatted with Dad, and I've had a word with Beth too.'

Beth is my social worker and she's always keen to be helpful. I hope she agrees with Mum.

'Beth suggested I talk to Jodi first – so I've had a little chat with her on the phone.'

Even though I know it's ridiculous, I get a twinge of jealousy that Mum got to speak to Jodi first. I wonder what she sounds like.

'I wanted to make sure she understands about you. I don't want her to put too much pressure on the meeting, for either of you.'

I know that Mum is just being Mum – cautious as usual and wanting to explain everything carefully – but I wish she would hurry up and get to the point! None of this matters to me. Jodi is my sister. I have to meet her – I must.

'But Jodi sounds lovely,' says Mum finally. 'I think you'll like her. She insists that she does understand. We've arranged for you to meet next weekend – on Sunday.'

21

'*Love will find a way*,' Sarah sings, as she gets me dressed. She doesn't have the most tuneful voice, but she makes up for it with enthusiasm. I'm still revelling in the news about meeting Jodi next weekend and I love the Glowlight song that Sarah's singing. The concert is tonight and she's extra smiley, clearly excited.

She wheels me out of my room for breakfast and something rustles beneath my wheels. Sarah gasps.

'Oh, Finn!' she says.

She turns me sideways so I can see that the hall floor is lined with neatly torn strips of newspaper, carefully arranged in rows. Finn is at the other end of the hall, but comes back swiftly, looking annoyed that my wheels have put a few strips out of place.

Dad comes downstairs. 'Finn!' he exclaims. 'I hope that's not today's paper. I haven't read it yet!'

The little strip near to my wheel with *Sat* on it gives him his answer. The paper is Dad's weekend treat – he doesn't have time to read one during the week. In fact, he often doesn't end up reading it on the weekend either, but I think he likes it being there.

Dad looks annoyed for a second, then laughs and Sarah joins in.

Then, when Mum goes to sit down at the table for a coffee, she jumps back up again, shouting 'Oww!' and clutching her bottom. From the chair, she picks up the spiky plant. Finn must have had enough of it. I bet he's moved the china elephant back to its normal spot too. The plant is squashed and misshapen and I think Finn and I are both glad when Mum throws it in the bin.

Sarah is getting all glammed up for the concert. She paints her nails with gold nail varnish. Then she does mine. It isn't easy as my hands like to curl up and my fingers are reluctant to stay straight. Muscle spasms make my arms and hands move about sometimes too. But Sarah is patient.

'Try to keep them still until they dry,' she tells me.

No amount of effort will give me control of my limb movements, but somehow my nails dry without too much smearing. I like the way the glint of gold catches my eye every time my head or hands move.

Now Sarah is doing her make-up. I watch as she carefully applies gold eyeshadow, black eyeliner and black mascara.

'I'll do yours in a minute,' she tells me.

She looks so glamorous – like a model. She hardly wears any make-up except on dates. I wonder what I will look like with make-up on.

Sarah carefully applies foundation to my skin with a sponge. It feels soft and cool.

'I'm not sure it's quite your colour, but it's near enough,' she says, turning me towards the mirror.

She looks at my eyes, thoughtfully. I soon have a sparkle of gold eyeshadow above my eyes. The mascara is a disaster, though, as I jolt and end up with smears of black on my cheek. As Sarah rubs at it I look like I have a black eye.

'If your mum came in now she'd think I'd been beating you up!' says Sarah. There is an edge to her voice despite the jokey tone.

The mascara cleaned off, Sarah starts again with more foundation. I wonder if she'll bother with mascara, but she does.

'Your eyelashes are longer than mine,' she says jealously.

I feel the soft grease of the lipstick as it brushes my lips.

'Look at you now!' She moves me round so I can see myself more clearly in the mirror.

I look so different. My head is still at a funny angle, my mouth gaping and not quite symmetrical – but I look older. I wish I could look like this when I meet Jodi. I look like someone about to head off for a Glowlight concert. I wish I was. I wish so much!

Sarah leaves me in the lounge with the telly on while she finishes getting ready.

Dad comes in, on his way up to read bedtime stories to Finn and Olivia.

I hope he'll say something nice about my make-up, but he doesn't even notice! Now I know how Mum feels whenever she gets her hair cut. Sometimes she says she's tempted to shave her head, just to see if he realises.

'You like Glowlight, don't you?' he says. 'I'll put some on for you.'

He turns off the telly and soon the sound of Glowlight fills the room, the song with the cool drum bit at the start. Mum calls to him to turn it down.

'We like it loud, don't we, Jemma?' says Dad. 'But we'd better keep your mum happy.' He smiles at me and then looks closer. 'Jemma! Is that make-up? You look great!'

I love the music. I absorb it – every note, every beat. I imagine I am there, with Sarah. My eyes close. Maybe this is better than really being there as in my mind I can clap and dance. I'm not in a wheelchair. I am just like everyone else.

The image of the band goes in and out of focus and the figures around me start to blur. The notes suddenly go off-key. I look down and see my wheelchair. I'm not dancing. And then the person in front of me turns round. A face looms closer.

'If I were you, I'd top myself.'

Dan's menacing grin. His cold eyes.

'I know you can't so I've come to give you a hand – put you out of your misery.'

Then I feel my chair being pushed. I need Sarah! Where is she? I can't see her.

I wake with a start.

Mum's standing over me, frowning. I'm breathing fast, but my breaths come slower as I take in that it was just a bad dream, that I'd nodded off.

'What's she done to you!' Mum exclaims. 'All that make-up!'

Sarah comes in. I get a lovely whiff of her perfume.

Mum takes Sarah to one side and speaks quietly to her. I try to hear what they're saying. Sounds like Mum's moaning about my make-up – saying it will take ages to clean off.

I wish I could tell Mum I enjoyed being made up and to lay off Sarah, for once.

'Enjoy the concert,' Mum tells her.

'Thanks – bye.' There is still a frostiness in Sarah's voice. She turns to me and smiles. 'Bye, Jemma! I'll tell you all about it tomorrow!'

I hear the front door close. She's gone.

22

In the morning, Mum gets me ready.

'Looks like Sarah's having a lie-in,' she tells me. 'Must have been a late one – I didn't even hear her come in.'

I realise I didn't hear her either – though I have a blurry memory of hearing a car outside.

At about half ten, Olivia comes running down.

'Sarah's not here! She's not in her room!'

'You shouldn't have gone in,' Dad scolds her. He goes up to look and comes back confirming Olivia is right.

'Told you.' Olivia pouts.

'She must be staying with one of the friends she went with to the concert,' says Mum.

'She could have let us know.' Dad sounds irritated. 'I'll text her, just to check she's OK.'

He does, but an hour later he's had no reply. 'Probably still asleep,' he says.

I'm trying not to panic, but I don't believe Sarah has gone back to Richard's. She sounded really certain when she said she doesn't want to be with him any more, so why would she?

Could Dan have found out about Richard – found out that Sarah was going to the concert with him? I feel like my worst fears are coming true.

Hours go by. I keep wishing Sarah would walk through the door, bubbly, pretending not to be hungover, full of what a great concert it was.

She doesn't.

Mum tries phoning Sarah, but says her phone seems to be switched off. 'She probably turned it off for the concert and forgot to put it on again,' says Mum. 'Or left her charger at home.'

By 4 p.m. Mum and Dad are both looking anxious.

'I don't even know who she was going with,' Mum comments. 'Was it Dan? Do you think we should try to call him? Or her friends . . . that Rihanna? Who's the other one – Emma, isn't it? But how would we get hold of them? All their numbers will be in Sarah's phone . . .'

'Shall we call the police?' says Dad.

'Let's give it a few more hours,' says Mum. 'She's

probably still hungover at Dan's or a friend's house – something like that.'

Mum doesn't sound sure that she believes what she's saying, even as she says it. I am even less sure.

A few more hours go by. Mum says she'll try looking at Sarah's laptop – see if she can find a number for Dan or one of her friends, but she comes down saying she can't get into anything without Sarah's password. She finds the phone number for Sarah's sister Kate, which Sarah gave her for emergencies. Dad phones Kate after dinner, but there's no answer. Then he phones the police.

'They took the details, but they didn't sound that interested,' he tells Mum. 'She's an adult – it's not like when we lost Finn.'

'It isn't like her to go off and say nothing, though,' says Mum.

'I did tell them that,' says Dad. 'I'll keep trying Kate. Sarah doesn't have any other family, does she?'

'No, her mum died years ago,' says Mum. 'I don't think there was anyone else.'

I'm facing towards the doorway and I can picture Sarah coming through, smiling and laughing. Then I see her at the concert, like she was in my dream. But as I try to fix the image of her in my mind, it fades. What happened, Sarah? Where are you? Did you get to the concert? Did Dan find out? Just come home, Sarah. Please.

23

I wake with a moment's calm on Monday and then my stomach drops when I remember that Sarah is missing. She's still not back. This is seriously worrying. And the police aren't even looking for her yet.

Mum gets me ready. She is gentle, but her face is weary, her eyes droopy. I don't think she's had much sleep.

The glint of my varnished nails keeps catching my eye. It feels like only moments ago that Sarah was putting it on me.

'Don't worry, Jemma. I'm sure Sarah will be home soon,' Mum tells me.

It doesn't feel right for me to swan off to school and carry on like normal. Olivia doesn't want to go either. She tries hiding the car keys, but when Mum quickly finds them she starts screaming.

'Dylan will kill me for breaking his tooth!' she yells.

'If you're worried about anything, tell a teacher,' Mum says. 'I'll come in with you and explain about Sarah – I'll tell them today is a difficult day for you.'

'I'm not going! I'm not going!' Olivia blubs.

The minibus is here to pick me up. I am wheeled out, leaving Olivia still in a tantrum.

We drive away from the house, but the same series of images runs through my mind. The frosty look Sarah gave Mum. The front door slamming as she left. Sarah at the concert, blurry figures around her. Is one of them Dan? Sarah and Richard – he's thrilled to be with her, she's worrying Dan will call. Sarah and Dan, him begging her to live with him. Sarah's phone beeping – always Dan's name.

A new thought hits me. Could she have planned this? Could she have run away with Dan?

The next image is Dan's sneering face as he watched Ryan's funeral on telly and told me no one would catch him. If she has run away with him, she's not safe.

At school I have swimming. It's a pain being changed and dried and changed back again, but it is always worth it. I am held in the water by Sheralyn, my volunteer helper, with the aid of some floats.

My arms and legs stretch out in the water. I feel free – floating and uncurling as if I'm moving through air. In my chair I feel heavy and unwieldy; it's hard for people to move me. In water a nudge is enough – I am as light as air and nothing presses into me at awkward angles. The water is so soft – softer even than my bed and so gentle. It feels delicious – the strongest sensation I experience apart from eating, and far more pleasurable.

I lie on my back in the pool and stare up at the panelled ceiling. I can see my reflection repeated in a number of mirrored tiles all at once as if there are three or four of me. The mirror reflects reality, but not quite. That is how things feel with Sarah – real, but not quite. She can't really have disappeared, can she?

The water is warm, but I get cold quickly. Sheralyn comments that my fingers are going white. It is time to come out. I like Sheralyn. She is very gentle. She's training to be a teacher and says she wants to teach 'people like me'. She's good, but she sometimes forgets to talk to me. Sometimes while they are changing us the volunteers start chatting to each other and forget that we are people who need to be talked to as well.

On the way home from school in the minibus I try to picture Sarah sitting in the living room. Running into the hall when I come through the door. I pray, even though I don't know if I believe in God.

'Please, God,' I say, 'please let Sarah be home.'

She is not.

Later, after dinner, Mum is putting Finn and Olivia to bed and I'm keeping Dad company in the kitchen while he washes up. The phone rings and he quickly dries his hands on a tea towel and grabs it.

I hold my breath. My heartbeat thuds in my ears.

'Oh – hello, Kate,' says Dad. 'You got my message?'

Maybe Kate knows something. Maybe Sarah's with her. I listen eagerly, but Dad takes the phone out of the room.

Mum comes running down the stairs. 'Who is it?' she says. 'Any news?'

'Kate only just saw the message,' says Dad as they both come back into the kitchen. 'She's not spoken to Sarah for about a month, but that's not unusual. They're not that close. She didn't sound too worried, though. She said Sarah's sometimes a bit impulsive. She went missing for a few days when she was a teenager. She'd gone off with some boy she fancied and not bothered to tell anyone.'

'She's not a teenager now, though,' Mum says doubtfully. 'She's a woman in her twenties with a job and responsibilities. If she wanted to go off with Dan, why wouldn't she just tell us? What do *you* think, Ben?'

Dad shrugs. 'It's hard to believe she'd go and leave all her stuff here.'

'Go where?' Olivia has appeared in the doorway in her nightie. 'You're talking about Sarah, aren't you? Where's she gone? Tell me.'

'Bedtime, Olivia,' says Dad. 'We're sure Sarah will be back soon.'

24

Sarah's been missing for three days. Mum and Dad are talking a lot in hushed whispers.

'Kate suggested we try her laptop again. She gave a few suggestions for passwords,' Dad tells Mum.

'I'll try,' says Mum. 'One of her mates must know where she is.'

The one person they need to contact is the one they won't even think of looking for. They need to speak to Richard.

Dad puts on a Disney film for us when we're all back from school. I don't feel like watching it. I want to do something – I want to help find Sarah.

Mum spends a while in Sarah's room. She comes down sighing.

'I checked and I'm sure all her stuff is still there, like we thought – her iPad, her clothes, her jewellery,' Mum says. 'I tried a few passwords for the laptop and would you believe it was "Jemma" and her birth date.'

I am Sarah's password! I get a painful ache in my chest. I wish they'd realise that I am also the real-life password to the information they need.

'Well done!' says Dad, impressed.

'I searched her contacts and Facebook friends, but I can't see Dan there, which is strange. She doesn't use email much,' Mum tells Dad. 'I guess it's all texts these days. But she'd sent messages to Rihanna and Emma. I've emailed both of them to see if they were with her on Saturday or if they know how to get in touch with Dan. The emails don't mention the concert, but one to Rihanna mentions what a "cow" I've been to her lately.' Mum's voice cracks slightly. 'I know we haven't been getting on brilliantly. Surely things weren't bad enough for her to walk out on us, though?'

'I don't think so,' says Dad.

I think about Dan trying to convince Sarah to leave me. She was tempted, I'm sure. She wasn't as happy here as she used to be.

The police arrive just after dinner. Two officers walk into the kitchen. They are both tall and with their uniforms the kitchen seems instantly too full. I see the man glance at me and then quickly look away, while the woman smiles as if she's ignoring the tense atmosphere. It's like the room itself is holding its breath.

'I'll put the television on for the children,' Mum tells them. I wonder if I am going to be dispatched to the living room with Finn and Olivia.

'Have you found Sarah?' Olivia asks the policewoman.

She shakes her head. 'We're trying our best,' she says, and then introduces herself to us as PC Sahin.

'You should look harder,' Olivia tells them. 'Dad found Finn with some chocolate finger biscuits. Maybe if we get something that Sarah really likes then that'll make her come back. I know! She loves Glowlight. Maybe if we put their music on – or maybe we can even get the band to come here and put an announcement on the telly. She won't want to miss that.'

'Thanks for your help,' PC Sahin says, smiling. 'It's nice to hear your ideas.'

'So will you do it, then?' Olivia demands.

'Come on, Olivia,' says Mum.

Olivia hesitates. She'd love to stay just as I would – but she loves TV too and follows Mum. Finn goes with them. The police officers sit down at the kitchen table. They smile at me, but seem unsure whether to speak to me.

'You must be worried about your carer,' says PC Sahin.

I certainly am. My head jolts back and an 'ughhh' noise comes out of me.

'Is she compos mentis?' the man, PC Hunt, asks Mum quietly as she comes back in.

'Oh yes, but she can't communicate. I wish she could – Sarah talks to her a lot.'

'Not much use to us, then,' PC Hunt mutters, screwing up his nose.

I wish I could kick him.

Mum looks at me and then makes tea for the police officers. She leaves me where I am. She's decided I should be in on this – maybe because Sarah is my carer or maybe she feels bad about what the policeman just said.

PC Hunt starts asking Mum questions. It's all background stuff – how long Sarah's been here, how the care is paid for. I have a question of my own: how is this going to help find her? Mum tells them about Dan, that she's been trying to get hold of him.

PC Hunt finally begins asking questions about the

night Sarah went missing. But of course all Mum knows is that Sarah was going to the concert. She doesn't know who with – she doesn't think it was Dan. Emma and Rihanna replied to Mum's email, but they didn't know about the concert and haven't heard from Sarah either. They also didn't know much about Dan.

'Most missing people reappear within forty-eight hours,' PC Sahin tells Mum. 'Now it is three days this is of course more concerning, but please try not to worry. We will pass the details to the Missing Persons Bureau, but we have classified her as "low risk". The most likely thing is still that she has gone off of her own accord – that she's with her boyfriend or some other friends.'

'I really don't know,' says Mum. 'Dan seems like a good sort to me. I don't see why they'd go off together without telling us.'

'We will try to trace Sarah's phone,' says PC Hunt, 'and also speak to Dan. It's a shame no one knows his last name.'

It seems shifty to me that he isn't on Facebook and Sarah's friends don't know him.

The doorbell rings while the police are still talking things through.

Mum goes to get the door, leaving the kitchen in

silence. I recognise the voice, even though I've only met him a few times. It's Richard. Is Sarah with him?

'Is Sarah in?' I hear him ask Mum.

'Oh . . . Richard,' says Mum. 'No, she's not –'

'Her phone's been off since the concert,' Richard interrupts. 'I'm a bit worried she's not been in touch. Maybe I did something to upset her?'

'She went to the concert with you?' says Mum.

'Yes! Who did you think she went with?' says Richard. Then he pauses. 'Wh-what's wrong?'

Mum lowers her voice as she explains to him what's happened. I can't hear his reaction, but the next moment Richard comes into the kitchen, blinking likes someone who's come into a bright room from somewhere dark.

He looks from PC Hunt to PC Sahin and back at Mum. He shuffles his feet. Then he glances back towards the front door as if he wishes he could make a fast getaway.

Mum explains to the police about Richard being with Sarah at the concert. Richard begins to babble.

'We met in town, went to the concert and afterwards I drove Sarah back here. She got out of the car and I watched her walk up the path to the front door. She had her door key out. I didn't wait for her to go inside. I drove off. Oh my God! How could something happen to her at the front door?'

'Do you remember what time you dropped her off?' PC Hunt asks him.

'Oh . . . let me think. It must have been about half eleven.'

'Are you sure she didn't come in and then go out again?' PC Sahin asks Mum.

'I didn't hear the door and it doesn't look like she changed or anything. I really don't think so.'

I know she didn't. I'd have heard the front door. But what Richard's saying sounds so unlikely – he brought her back and she *disappeared* before coming inside. Can that really be true?

PC Sahin turns to Richard. 'And you didn't have any kind of row? She wasn't upset?'

'No, we had a great time. She's always smiling, Sarah. I don't think I've seen her upset in the ten months we've been going out! We've never rowed – I can tell you that.'

I see Mum's eyebrows shoot up to her hairline. Her mouth drops open. She's not sure what to say. As far as she's concerned they split up three months ago, when Sarah started going out with Dan.

PC Hunt turns to Mum. 'I thought you said her boyfriend was called Dan?'

'Dan?' Richard repeats. 'Who's Dan?'

Mum's hand covers her eyes as if she wishes she could hide. She slowly takes a breath and then looks at Richard.

Richard's mouth is taut as Mum explains about Dan, his eyes still, staring at her and then at the wall.

'I don't believe it . . . I don't believe it.' His eyes are glassy now.

He's being so dramatic I begin to wonder if he knew already.

I'd been worrying so much that Dan would find out about Richard, but what if Richard found out about Dan? Does that change things?

'You appear to be last person who saw her, then,' says PC Sahin.

25

There is still no news about Sarah. Four days. That's double the time they said missing people usually turn up in.

Finn is doing his head-banging thing more and more, and Olivia is having even more tantrums than usual. Mum's put the TV on for them and they're quiet for the time being, watching a kids' series about aliens. I'm in the kitchen keeping Mum company while she cooks dinner. She seems to like having me close to her at the moment. I don't think she likes being alone. Or maybe she's worried about how I'm feeling without Sarah.

Someone rings at the door and Mum hurries to open it. I hear Paula's voice.

'Lorraine! I heard about Sarah. The police came to speak to us. What do you think has happened to her?'

'Come in, Paula,' Mum says. 'Have a cup of tea.' Mum catches my eye as she leads Paula into the kitchen, with a look that says she could have done without Paula turning up.

'The police think she's gone off somewhere of her own accord,' Mum says, pulling out a chair.

Paula sits down.

'You don't mind if I carry on?' Mum says, pointing to the chopping board, full of waiting carrots.

'They said that when I first reported Ryan missing,' says Paula. Mum stares at her and then glances at me.

But Paula doesn't seem to take the hint. 'I said to Graeme, it's strange that the police should come to us. Only a few doors apart. And so soon after my Ryan . . .'

There's a loud snap as Mum chops a carrot with extra force. I see her breathe in and compose herself. 'Paula, I'm not sure what you're –'

'Do you think they're linked? It . . . it can't just be a coincidence.'

Paula gives me an awkward glance – she's clearly wondering if she should be saying all this in front of me. I swallow. I want her to keep talking. Even though what she's implying has happened to Sarah is making my chest hurt, I want them to realise there is a connection – Dan and Sarah, Dan and Ryan. Dan.

But looking from Mum to Paula, my heart sinks. The desperation in Paula's eyes. Mum will just think it's Paula's grief – that she's trying to make things fit together so she can have an answer.

'They're speaking to everyone on the street,' Mum says, softly but firmly. 'Richard says Sarah got out of his car just outside the house around half past eleven on Saturday night. The police want to know if anyone heard or saw anything.'

'Yes,' says Paula. 'That's what they asked us. But we're both on sleeping tablets, you see. Don't get a wink otherwise – not since . . . you know. Do you really think she just went off?'

'I don't know what to think,' says Mum. She pours tea for Paula and then goes back to chopping the carrots loudly. 'Have you had any news yourselves, about . . . about Ryan?'

Paula sighs deeply and runs her finger round the rim of her mug.

'Nothing,' she says. 'I got my hopes up when they charged that Jay. He was Ryan's regular dealer, and they had a falling out about money or something. But Jay was out of town – he proved it. The more time goes by the less likely I think it is that they'll get him.' She looks up. 'Though perhaps now . . .'

The doorbell rings again.

'Goodness, we're popular tonight!' Mum exclaims.

She turns a pan down on the stove and excuses herself. The smell of mince frying wafts over me as she goes out into the hall.

Paula meets my eye briefly for a moment and looks as if she might say something, but then thinks better of it. People do that a lot.

Mum's voice is loud with surprise as she opens the front door.

'Oh, Dan . . .' I hear her say.

26

I can't believe he's here. I feel suddenly cold, so cold.

Mum is talking to him as he follows her into the kitchen. 'We wanted to call you,' she's saying, 'but we couldn't find your number.'

'Call me? Why? Has something happened?' Dan asks, as he comes into the room. 'I –' He stops when he sees Paula. He doesn't look at me at all. 'Paula, this is Dan – Sarah's boyfriend,' says Mum. She runs her hand across her brow. Her eyes are wide with shock. If Dan's here that means Sarah's not run off with him.

Paula nods.

'Dan, this is my neighbour, Paula,' Mum continues.

Dan nods back. Does he realise who Paula is?

'What's going on?' Dan asks. 'Sarah's phone's been off. I came over to see her.'

'Oh, Dan,' says Mum, her voice shaking. 'She isn't here. We haven't seen her since Saturday. Have you not heard from her at all?'

'No. What's going on?'

Dan turns his head to look at Mum and I can't see his face. I wish I could. Surely his expression would give him away.

Paula stands up, her chair scraping the floor noisily in her haste. 'I'd better be going,' she says. 'I do hope she turns up.'

'Turns up?' Dan repeats. He looks at Paula and I see a crease spread across his forehead. I watch him closely. He definitely looks surprised to hear that Sarah is missing. There are beads of sweat on his forehead. Does he really know nothing or is this all an act?

'I'll see Paula off then I'll tell you everything, Dan,' Mum says.

For a moment I am alone with Dan. I wish he'd say something – confide in me. I watch him. His hands don't keep still – he's rubbing his fingers together.

Mum is back. Phlegm clogs my throat and I cough.

'Dan, the police have been looking for you,' Mum tells him.

He seems nervous now, his feet shuffling. His eyes flash in alarm.

'What? Why?' he asks.

'You haven't seen or heard from her then, Dan –

not since Saturday? We thought she might have been with you . . .'

Dan shakes his head. 'No.'

'Sarah was at a concert on Saturday night and didn't come back here. No one's seen her since. Sit down, Dan – this must be a shock. I'll make you a tea.'

Dan moves towards a chair and leans on the back of it, but he doesn't sit down. 'A concert? I thought she was working last weekend.'

It's Mum's turn to shuffle about awkwardly.

I look at Dan. I'm sure this is an act. He's challenging Mum to confirm what he knows – that Sarah was two-timing him.

'She went with a friend – actually, her ex, Richard. I think he must have got tickets for it ages ago. She probably felt she had to go – you know what she's like!'

'Right,' says Dan, with an edge to his voice. 'So I assume the police have been questioning him, then?'

'Yes,' Mum says. 'He was the last person to see her, but I don't think they . . . They want to speak to you too. You'll call them, won't you?'

Dan's gaze is steady. 'Of course,' he says.

27

I spend all the next day wondering what will happen when Dan talks to the police. He has to call them, doesn't he? But one thing we know now is that Sarah hasn't run off with him. Could she have left on her own? Would she really do that? Or has something else happened – something I can't bear to even think about?

When I get home from school, I'm surprised to find Sheralyn, my swimming volunteer, waiting for me. Mum says when she told the head teacher at my school what had happened, she said Sheralyn might be able to help out as she's done care work before. It turns out she's still registered with the agency Mum uses and she was keen to help. I'm glad it's Sheralyn, but at the same time having her here only makes me want Sarah back more, if that's possible. Sarah has been missing for five days.

Sheralyn decides to take me for a walk to the

shopping centre. Maybe she's trying to take my mind off things, but I hate the shopping centre. Too many people staring. They either look appalled or desperately sorry for me. There's always some kid with a finger up one nose pointing at me with the other hand and saying, 'What's wrong with her?' Sarah used to bring me here a lot, but I think she sensed all the comments were upsetting me and we stopped coming so often.

As we reach the shops I recognise a man who is walking towards us. It's Dan's friend Billy. I see him look and recognise me, but he just walks straight past. It's the total opposite to what he was like before. Of course, he doesn't know Sheralyn, but would it hurt to stop and say hello?

As we reach the more crowded shopping area, I start thinking about my sister. She doesn't live that far away. What if she was here, now, walking round the shops? I wonder if I would recognise her from the photo. I'm looking at every girl and wondering if she could be her. That girl with dark hair looks too tall. This one has a kind face but her hair is too light.

Ahead there is a woman with blond hair, tied back in a ponytail, walking away from us. My heart suddenly skips a beat. *Sarah*. She looks like Sarah. She really could be – she could be Sarah! She's walking faster than us – she's disappearing into the crowd. Wait!

She doesn't wait. She's gone. It couldn't have been Sarah, could it? If she's run away, she wouldn't still be round here. She'd be worried about being spotted. I don't think she walked quite like Sarah either. I have a lingering hope, though. Maybe it was her. Maybe she's on her way home. Perhaps she's popped into the shops to buy some flowers – or something to give Mum, to give all of us, to say sorry for all the worry she's caused.

She doesn't need to say sorry to me. I'd forgive her for getting us all so worried if she only came home.

'Hey – wait!' a woman calls. Sheralyn stops and swings me round. The woman has short grey hair. She must be sixty or seventy. What does she want?

'Here, take this for the poor lass,' the woman says. She holds out a ten-pound note.

I can't see Sheralyn's face, as she is pushing me, but I hear the shock in her voice.

'No – really, that's very kind, but –'

'Please, dear,' says the woman. 'I insist – take it.'

The money has gone from the woman's hand. I'm not a charity. Sarah would never have done that. She would have explained that I am well looked after

– that I have what I need. I don't need strangers giving me money in the street. I'm not a desperate homeless person.

'Sorry, Jemma,' Sheralyn says quietly as the woman disappears in the crowd. 'That was so embarrassing. I didn't know what to say. I'll put the money in a charity box.'

When we get back, I am still feeling cross about the woman treating me like a charity case. Mum's upstairs with Finn and Olivia but Sheralyn takes over with them and Mum comes down. She's holding something – a letter!

'Jemma, I've got another letter for you from Jodi,' she says.

I can feel my heart beating faster as Mum begins to read.

'*Dear Jemma,*

'*This is just a short note to say I am so excited about meeting you on Sunday! I can't wait and I can't think about anything else! Your mum was so lovely on the phone – she's told me all about you. I hope you are as excited as I am! I'm counting the days and the hours and the minutes!*

'*Love, Jodi x x x.*'

Mum folds the letter and looks at me.

'Jemma, I'd forgotten we arranged this. I wonder if we should postpone it . . .'

'No!' I want to yell. I know everything with Sarah is awful, but I want to meet Jodi so much. I need something good to happen and this is going to be it. I must meet my sister.

'Then again,' says Mum, 'we don't want to let Jodi down. This is such a big deal for both of you. Maybe it will take your mind off things.'

Mum sighs. I'm relieved. I just hope she doesn't change her mind again.

When I get back from school the next day, Olivia's already home and she's jumping up and down with excitement. My heart races. Is it Sarah – is she back? I've been full of excitement myself all day about meeting Jodi on Sunday, but Olivia can't be excited about that.

'Guess what?' she says, bounding up to me. 'I took a photo of Sarah to school and I showed it round to see if anyone had seen her – and Ruby Jones says she saw her in Tesco!'

'Don't get your hopes up too high, Olivia,' Mum

says gently. 'It was probably someone who looks like Sarah.'

So Sarah is not back. I get a pang of guilt for feeling happy about meeting Jodi when Sarah is still missing.

'It was her,' Olivia insists. 'Ruby said she was sure! You weren't there so how can you know?'

'It might have been Sarah that Ruby saw,' Mum acknowledges. 'It also might not.'

'It was her,' Olivia insists again.

I wish it was. I wish so much that it was Sarah who Ruby saw in Tesco and that I saw in the shopping centre.

During dinner, the phone rings. Dad answers it.

'Oh, Kate! Hello,' he says. 'Any news? How are you coping?'

'Tell her Ruby saw Sarah,' Olivia demands. 'She'll want to know. You must tell her.'

'Shhhh! Wait,' Mum whispers. 'Let's find out why she's rung first.'

'You have? Really?' says Dad. 'Do any of them seem likely?'

Likely? What could that mean?

I can't see Dad's face, but I can see how eagerly Mum and Olivia are watching him. Finn is tapping his fork on his plate. *Tap, tap, tap*, over and over.

I wish he'd stop.

Dad says something about a card. And then, 'That's typical.'

'What's she saying?' Olivia demands. 'Have they found Sarah or what? Tell her about Ruby. Ruby saw her!'

'Shhhh!' Mum tells her, putting her finger to her lips.

'That sounds like an excellent idea,' Dad continues, after listening for a few moments. 'Of course we'll help in any way we can. Just let us know.'

He puts the phone down. Mum looks at him questioningly.

'Why didn't you tell her?' Olivia shouts. She stands up and kicks her chair over.

'Stop that, Olivia!' Dad says firmly. 'Sit down and listen if you want to know what Kate said.'

Olivia hesitates, but she does want to know. She picks up her chair and sits down.

'Kate's started a social media campaign and she's already had a few people contact her with sightings,' Dad tells Mum.

'See – I told you Ruby saw her!' Olivia interrupts. 'I told you and you didn't believe it.'

'The first few didn't sound likely,' Dad continues, 'but now there've been three quite close together – all within ten miles of here – that do sound possible. The most interesting news is that the police say Sarah's cash card was used two days ago to withdraw a hundred pounds – and the cashpoint is in Watford, not far from those three sightings.'

Sarah's taken money from a cashpoint. That must mean she's alive, mustn't it? Or is this Dan trying to throw people off the scent?

'Goodness,' says Mum. 'Was there CCTV at the cashpoint?'

'The camera near the cashpoint wasn't working and they couldn't see anyone matching her description on the other nearby cameras – though they're still going through the footage. The police think it's a good sign. Her phone was last used at the concert itself so that hasn't been much help. Kate is certainly hopeful, though.'

'It was her,' says Olivia firmly.

'Kate's put Sarah's details on the Missing People charity web page. If someone doesn't want to be found they can still leave a message on there, just so family and friends know they are OK. She's getting some posters done and she's asked if we'll help put them up around here.'

'I'll help!' says Olivia.

If Sarah's been seen, if she's used a cashpoint, then it truly sounds possible that she chose to leave. I want her to be alive even though it's hard to bear the thought that she left us like that – that she was so unhappy. I can't bear this much longer, this limbo.

Later, Mum gets out the nail polish remover and takes off my now chipped nail varnish. I keep thinking about Sarah putting it on me so carefully, so kindly. I can see her sparkly eyes, her excitement about the concert. I don't want Mum to take it off – it connects me to Sarah and without it I feel like Sarah is even further away. But soon the nail varnish has gone and only the strong smell of the remover lingers, making me cough. I wonder if anyone will ever paint my nails again.

28

It is a week since Sarah went missing. *A whole week*.

Kate has come down with piles of posters and we are going round the streets putting them up. I've never met Kate before. She doesn't look like Sarah. She is much shorter and her face is narrower. Her hair is dark and Sarah's is fair. She has lines on her face. She looks much older than Sarah.

'Hi, Jemma, nice to meet you,' she says, smiling a little awkwardly. I jolt at the way she speaks. Her voice is so similar it could be Sarah.

Dad wasn't sure about all of us coming, but Olivia was determined to help.

I am 'parked' in front of a lamp post where the first poster has been stuck. It is weird seeing Sarah's face smiling down. Is she smiling somewhere now? I can't picture what she's doing, where she might be. It's just a blank. Kate seems so confident that the sightings were really her and that she's alive. Could it be true? Could it?

Dad asks Kate if the police have followed up the sightings and the cashpoint.

'They're still not sure if it was her,' Kate admits, 'but there's no proof that it wasn't, either.'

'And Ruby Jones saw her too!' Olivia pipes up.

'Yes, so you said,' says Kate. 'Any sighting might help – it's good that she told you.'

Once the posters are up, I am disappointed to see most people going past without even looking at them. If they look at all it is such a quick glance that they can't really take in her face – can they?

Sheralyn is with me and is supposed to be watching Finn too. To make him feel useful Dad has given him a wad of posters to hold, while Olivia is handing Dad bits of tape. Sheralyn is watching Olivia. No one apart from me has noticed that Finn is now lining up his posters neatly on the pavement against the fence. He has more than I thought – at least ten faces of Sarah staring up from the ground – and I can see what's going to happen. It's not that windy, but it will only take a bit of a breeze. Please, Sheralyn – look back! Look at Finn!

She does – but too late. A gust lifts the corner of one sheet, then another and suddenly they are all flittering up in the air – spreading across the pavement.

Finn lets out an anguished cry and starts flapping his arms – his neat work undone.

'Oh! Finn!' Sheralyn exclaims.

He makes no effort to pick them up – just watches as Sheralyn, Dad and Olivia quickly try to gather them. Some are flapping into the road like injured birds. Olivia runs to the edge of the kerb.

'Olivia – not in the road!' Dad yells, and to my relief Olivia stops.

A car runs over a poster and even from here I can see tyre marks on it.

'I could have got that one!' Olivia tells Dad crossly.

Mum and Kate are further down the road. I can't see them, but I hear Kate's voice. They must have seen and come back to help. I only see Kate when she steps into the road and retrieves the poster with the tyre marks. She stands on the pavement in front of me, staring at it and brushing it with her hand, as if the tyre marks might rub off. Tears run down her face.

As we head home, it begins to rain – just to make everyone more miserable – and no one has an umbrella. Although they are in plastic sleeves, the posters will be dripping and bedraggled before anyone even sees them. Mum and Sheralyn struggle to get my shower-proof cape over me, but I am already very wet. The chill dampness has seeped through to my skin, making me shiver. Raindrops tickle my face like insects and I wish I could wipe them away.

When we reach the house, Mum says Kate can't go home on the train all that way, soaked through. She insists she lend her some clothes and invites Kate to stay for dinner.

Once I am in dry clothes, Sheralyn leaves me in the living room with some music playing, saying she's going to have a shower. Kate, Mum and Dad are in the kitchen and I wish she'd taken me in there.

I'm sitting here, almost asleep, when Olivia slips in, unusually quietly for her. She goes over to Mum's handbag, which is on the sofa, opens the zip and starts rummaging. I wonder briefly if Mum has asked her to fetch something from her bag – but it's unlikely. Olivia keeps glancing towards the door too – so she's obviously doing something she shouldn't.

She doesn't seem to have realised that I'm here. I watch as she pulls out mum's purse and takes out a ten-pound note. She folds it and presses it quickly into her pocket. She zips up Mum's bag, then glances up at me – she meets my eyes, but then looks quickly away and hurries off.

What does Olivia want ten pounds for? Then I remember Mum saying money was missing from her purse. It was Olivia all along.

'Sarah was a bit on the wild side as a teenager – she had a string of hopeless boyfriends,' Kate tells us over dinner.

'Not much change there, then,' I want to say.

'And like I said,' Kate continues, 'I tried to warn her off this one lad and she got the hump and went off with him for a few days.'

'But she hasn't gone off with Dan – or with Richard,' Mum points out. 'They've both been here and are clearly worried about her.'

'I know,' says Kate.

There's a silence and I feel them all thinking about the other possibilities that no one wants to mention – the bad things that could have happened to her.

When Kate leaves after we've eaten I miss her voice. I miss her voice that sounds so much like Sarah.

29

We pass one of our posters as Mum drives me to the Family Centre where the meeting with Jodi has been arranged. I had imagined we'd meet in a café or something like that, but Mum says this will be more private and Jodi will have a social worker there to support her if she needs someone to talk to afterwards. Whatever I feel after this meeting will have to stay inside me. I can't share it. I hope it will go OK.

I am starting to feel sick as we go over road humps. I'm relieved that it is not a long journey and I am soon out of the car and being pushed by Mum up the ramp of a modern building that looks like a nursery school.

Mum speaks to someone at the reception desk and we are directed to the back of the building. Is Jodi here already?

We've arrived first and have to sit in a room similar to a doctor's waiting room. It's all making this feel so formal. Mum pulls me near her and squeezes my hand. I am grateful. I know she is nervous too. Then after a few minutes a woman with an ID on a chain comes bustling up to us, smiling.

'I'm Donna,' she tells us. 'I'm a social worker. Jodi is on her way. Would you like to come through to the room we've set up for you?'

Mum nods.

'Can I get you a coffee while you're waiting?'

'Thanks, that would be lovely,' says Mum.

'Would you like anything, Jemma?'

'No, she's fine,' says Mum.

Fine? I'm not sure about that!

The room is cosy with armchairs and a stripy rug, but the pale lime green walls and shiny plastic floor still look like a doctor's surgery. There is a landscape picture on the wall of fields and farm buildings and a scarecrow. It looks like a beautiful day – the sky is so blue and there are lots of shadows on the ground. I stare at the picture. It is calming.

'I hope she won't be long,' says Mum, looking at her watch and bringing me back to now. I wish I could have stayed with the picture. I've been excited until now, but I'm suddenly feeling really shaky inside.

It is a few minutes before Donna brings the coffee.

She goes out, leaving Mum clutching the mug as if for warmth, though it's not cold in here. She's anxious too – wondering if she's done the right thing, whether this is a good idea. She couldn't change her mind now, could she?

Donna is back, smiling. 'She's here! She's just popped to the loo. Bit nervous, I think!'

'I'm sure Jemma must be nervous too,' says Mum.

'You mustn't worry, though,' Donna tells me. 'We won't get in the way, but we'll both be here, on hand if needed.' She winks. It reminds me of Dan winking – though it is a very different wink. I'm sure this wink is saying 'good luck' rather than 'I'll be back to kill you sometime'. It makes me slightly uneasy, though. Mum and Donna move their chairs towards the far wall so Jodi and I will have some space. I can't see them now as I'm facing the door.

Then the door opens slowly and a girl comes in. She glances past me towards Mum and I hear Donna say warmly, 'Come on in, Jodi. This is Jemma.'

Jodi walks towards me and stands still. We stare at each other. She is a prettier than her photo, with short dark hair and a fluffy black jumper. The shock is – she looks far more like me than I'd realised. Our hair, dark eyes, small noses and pale, thin lips are so similar. My face looks as if it has been squashed in sideways. It is distorted, my features out of alignment. Yet I can see myself in her. We are so alike! She is shocked too. I can see it. Her mouth has dropped slightly open.

I wish she'd speak and I wish she'd sit down. She's standing too still – for too long. I think she's frozen.

'Oh – Jemma,' she says, at last.

I love it – I love hearing her say my name. My sister saying my name! I wait for more.

Her face creases up. She bursts into tears.

'I'm so sorry, Jemma. I can't do this!' she sobs.

Her hands cover her tear-stained face. I hadn't noticed the make-up until now when I see it smearing down her cheeks.

I want to reassure her – tell her to sit down, not to worry. I realise my delight in seeing the likeness between us has had the opposite effect on her. She is horrified to be so alike to someone so deformed. I'd normally be angry, but I can't – I'll forgive her anything if she'll just talk to me. She's my sister. My sister.

Donna rushes over. 'Jodi, why don't you sit down for a minute? I can understand this being a bit overwhelming. I'll get you a tissue.'

But Jodi doesn't sit.

'Jodi?' Mum tries.

'Stop crying, stop crying, please!' I want to beg her.

But suddenly the door has opened and shut and, in a blur, she has gone.

30

Donna hurries after her and a few moments later Mum follows.

I am alone. I don't think I've ever felt as alone as in this moment. I only had a sister for about two minutes but now there is a gaping gap in my life. She's gone. If this is what she meant about a missing piece, then I now understand. I'm missing her. But I was not her missing piece. Like Mum feared, I was not what Jodi was looking for. She's had a glimpse and I don't fit the gap in her puzzle.

I'm not alone for long, of course. Mum rushes back in and hugs me. My face is wet. I realise it is Mum crying, but when she finally lets go of me my face gets wetter still. I am crying too.

'Donna's talking to her now,' Mum says. 'She might calm down and come back in, but it's possible she might not. I'm so sorry, Jemma.'

We wait. Mum strokes my hand. We wait more.

I stare at the picture – the sunshine and the shadows. She will come back. She'll calm down. Donna will talk to her. She'll come back in.

We wait – and wait. Mum looks out into the corridor.

'They're still in that room,' she tells me. 'That's surely a good sign. You still want to see her, Jemma, don't you?' Mum looks at me closely. 'Maybe we should've waited until you could communicate. It's not fair on you. It would've been easier for Jodi too.'

Maybe Mum's right – but who knows how long that's going to take, and if it will ever happen. I don't want to wait for that. I want to see Jodi now. I can't bear that she's so close – across that corridor – and yet so, so far away.

Come back, Jodi! Please come back.

The door across the corridor bangs. The bang echoes down the hallway. Mum hesitates – unsure whether to go out to see what's happened or to wait. Our door opens. Donna comes in. She is alone. My heart sinks.

'I am so sorry,' Donna says, her voice low and grim, the opposite of the buzzy chirp she met us with earlier. She carries on talking about how bad Jodi feels, but I am feeling too sad to listen.

'Is she still here?' Mum asks hopefully. 'Maybe I can talk to her?'

Donna shakes her head, and my heart sinks down my legs and under my wheels. She's gone. It's like she's closed the door on me.

She came, she took one look and she went. That was my sister.

Back at home, I'm in a daze as Dad wheels me into the living room. I can see he has been playing Connect 4 with Olivia while Finn lines up matchsticks along the wall. Finn is wearing a helmet as he's been head-banging so much lately. Mum told Dad what happened with Jodi and then said she had a migraine and needed to lie down.

'I think we need to build a nest for Jemma,' Dad tells Olivia.

'A nest?' Olivia asks. 'What do you mean?'

'Jemma's had a hard morning and needs a bit of TLC. We'll stack up as many cushions as we can find into a nest and Jemma can sit in it and feel soft and safe and warm.'

'Can I sit in it too?' Olivia asks.

'After Jemma's had a turn you certainly can,' says Dad.

Dad got into this 'nesting' years ago when I was about five. He used to make nests for me all the time. It's a long time since he's made me one. I thought I'd grown out of them, but the thought of him doing this for me fills me with warmth and love and I realise I'm yearning to be snuggled and safe.

Olivia and Dad get busy with cushions.

I count as they pile up the cushions. They get up to ten in the end. Olivia stands back as Dad eases me gently into it. Even Finn pauses for a moment and looks up as I am lowered into the softness.

'How's that?' Dad asks.

I am held, nestled, caressed by the comforting cushions – though I can't be left alone in it in case I roll or cushions fall over me and I can't breathe.

'Is it my turn now?' Olivia asks.

'Let Jemma have some time in it first,' Dad tells her.

I expect her to protest.

'She does look cosy,' Olivia acknowledges.

I'd smile at her if I could.

My nest is so comfy and I can feel Dad's warmth and even Olivia's too – but I'm still so sad inside. I'm missing Sarah so much, and I want my sister to come back. I want Jodi.

*

An hour later I am back in my wheelchair. Olivia had a turn in the nest after me. Finn showed no interest, though I think he would be in it in a shot if no one was here. Dad has gone upstairs to check on Mum.

Finn is still lining up matchsticks, while Olivia is lining up all the dolls on the top floor of her doll's house and then knocking them one by one out of the window, saying, '*Wheeeeeee! Thump* – you're dead!'

I half watch her, but not closely as my mind is elsewhere. I am thinking about Jodi. Her face is imprinted on my mind – her likeness – the connection between us. Did Jodi feel it? Maybe she did and it was so strong it overwhelmed her. I wonder what she's doing right now, how she's feeling.

I realise after a bit that I can't see Finn or Olivia. I'm not sure if they've left the room or are out of sight behind me, but then I hear an unhappy grunting sound that must be Finn.

The sound is coming from behind me. Finn suddenly lurches past.

'Get back here,' Olivia says, but Finn is wriggling towards the door. He scrambles past me hotly pursued by Olivia. She tries to grab him, but he is out of the room in a flash. Poor Finn. I want to protect him. If I could move my legs I'd love to give Olivia a gentle sisterly kick. If I could talk, I'd ask her what's bothering her, and maybe she'd tell me, like she told me about Dylan.

Olivia holds her head up high and struts out.

As I sit alone thinking, I start to feel achy. I hope it's just the worry making this happen and that I'm not going to be ill. That's all I need.

There's a sudden piercing scream from upstairs.

'What's happened?' I hear Dad demanding.

'Finn headbutted me with his helmet!' Olivia screeches. 'I think he's cracked my head open!' She is wailing.

Maybe Finn can stand up for himself after all.

Later in the evening when Finn and Olivia are in bed, Dad wheels me into the living room. We find Mum in there, curled up in my nest, looking cosy, eating a bar of chocolate.

31

I feel wiped out and I don't want to go to school. The minibus arrives and Sheralyn comes with me as today is swimming.

The pool is not as warm today as it should be. I float, but I don't enjoy it. I feel shivery. Last week at swimming Sarah had only been missing a day. I was sure she'd be back when I got home. Now I'm scared she's really not coming back. I thought with the posters and Kate's campaign and the cash card that she might be found, but there's been no more news at all.

Back at home, the phone rings while we are eating dinner. If the phone rang during dinner the rule used to be that no one answered it. The person could leave a message. Now that rule is constantly broken. The phone rings much more often than it did too. Dad jumps up and answers it.

'Yes,' he says.

Then I see the colour drain from his face as he

listens. I can't swallow. It's Sarah. It has to be about Sarah. Mushed carrot sits in my mouth and a little spills out. Sheralyn doesn't notice. She's looking at Dad. We all are – apart from Finn, who is busy trying to line up the carrot sticks on his plate.

'One minute,' says Dad. He gives Mum a look and goes out into the hall with the phone.

'What's happened?' Olivia demands. 'Is Sarah dead? Did someone murder her? How did they do it? Was it a knife or a gun or did they strangle her?'

'Olivia!' Mum bellows in horror. 'Be quiet!'

'I want to know!' Olivia protests.

Some mushed carrot has dripped on to my pale cream top.

I am sure I hear Dad swear out in the hall. I don't think I've ever heard him swear before. The news must be bad.

'Ooh, yuck! Look at Jemma!' Olivia cries, screwing up her face.

Sheralyn and Mum both turn to me quickly.

'Oh – sorry, Jemma,' Sheralyn says, anxiously glancing from me to Mum, who has jumped up already to grab some kitchen towel.

'Here,' Mum says, passing it to Sheralyn.

Dad comes back in. He looks pale and his eyes look deeper than usual and darker.

'What's happened?' Olivia demands. 'Is Sarah dead?'

Finn bangs his head on the table.

'Shall I take them upstairs?' Sheralyn asks.

Finn goes with her, but Olivia refuses.

'I suppose you'll have to know sometime,' Dad sighs. 'That was Kate on the phone. The police have found a body. They've not identified it yet, but we have to prepare ourselves – they think it might be Sarah.'

I feel giddy. I was half expecting this and yet I wasn't. I wasn't at all.

Olivia begins to cry.

'It might not be her,' Mum tells us.

Dad hugs Olivia, who clings to him as she sobs in his arms.

I wish someone would hug me. Then Mum touches my shoulder and turns me to face her.

'Oh, Jemma,' she says gently and she squeezes my hand. I am so grateful – so relieved that she can sense my pain.

'Where . . . where did they find . . . the body?' she asks Dad.

'In Fox Woods,' Dad says. 'Kate's coming

tomorrow to identify her. I'm relieved that they didn't ask us to do it.' I see him shudder.

Olivia pulls away from Dad, her eyes red and face wet. Dad's shirt has a big wet patch too.

Mum goes and gives Olivia a squeeze, her eyes meeting Dad's. They know they can't promise us that it will be OK.

Later, when Olivia and Finn are in bed, I hear Dad talking to Mum. He says they told Kate the circumstances 'look suspicious'.

They've found a body; Dan must have killed her – he must have done. However much I try to think of a different explanation, I keep coming back to it. He killed Ryan and now he's killed Sarah. And he taunted me with it. I can rage all I want – I can hate him more than anything, but it makes no difference. He knew he could do what he wanted.

I knew all along what he was like.

And now it's too late.

32

When the doorbell rings after dinner I'm sure it's him – come to taunt me again – the keeper of his secret. Mum and Dad are upstairs, so Sheralyn goes out of the living room to answer it. I hear her say, 'Can I help you?'

But it's not Dan; it's Richard.

He jabbers nervously. 'Is Lorraine here? I . . . I'm Sarah's . . . I don't even know what to call myself – boyfriend, friend, ex-boyfriend – one of those . . . I'm sorry . . . I don't . . . Who are you?'

Olivia sneaks out into the hall to see what's going on, just as Sheralyn explains that she is standing in for Sarah as my carer.

'I'll call Lorraine – she's upstairs,' Sheralyn tells him. 'Lorraine! Sarah's boyfriend is here,' she calls loudly.

'He's not her boyfriend – Dan is!' Olivia blurts out. 'He's not been her boyfriend for ages! Why are you pretending to be Sarah's boyfriend?'

'I'm not pretending. It's complicated,' Richard explains. He sniffs.

'Anyway, Sarah's dead!' Olivia blurts out.

There's another loud sniff and Richard tries to speak, but Olivia interrupts him.

'You're crying. Men don't cry.'

'Olivia! Go back in the lounge,' Sheralyn tells her.

'Won't!' Olivia says with her usual stubborn tone.

'Please, Olivia – now!' says Sheralyn.

'I'm only telling the truth – so why should I be punished?' Olivia protests.

It's Mum to the rescue as she comes downstairs and invites Richard through to the kitchen.

'I'm sorry to drop in like this,' he says. 'The police came round. They've been asking more questions . . .'

Richard's voice disappears into the kitchen. I strain to catch anything – try to tune out all other sounds – but it's no use.

My bag needs emptying. If Sheralyn takes me to the bathroom there's a good chance I will hear something. I want her to notice, but she is still busy arguing with Olivia.

'I'm going upstairs,' Olivia says finally. She seems

to be expecting Sheralyn to protest, but Sheralyn says nothing and Olivia storms out and up the stairs.

I see Finn's clenched hand on the sofa relax as she leaves the room.

'I'll take Jemma to the toilet and then I'll be back,' Sheralyn tells him.

As she pushes me in and turns me I see that she hasn't fully closed the door. I strain my ears to hear.

'We don't know for sure that it's her,' says Mum.

'They think I k–' says Richard. He swallows. 'They think I've done something to her. They keep asking me – am I sure she got to the door, what did I do when I got home, can anyone confirm I was there?'

'No one saw you get home, then?' Mum asks.

'I live on my own,' says Richard. 'Nobody saw me go into my flat.' He's babbling now, as his voice chokes up. 'I love Sarah so much. I'd never hurt her. I'm not like that. I'd never hurt anyone.'

'I'm sure you wouldn't,' says Mum. I can hear Richard crying again.

'Anyway,' says Mum, 'we'll have to wait until the body's been identified. The police can't have any evidence against you or they'd have arrested you, wouldn't they?'

Sheralyn is taking longer than usual. She must be eavesdropping too. Now the conversation seems to be ending she wheels me back quickly to the living room.

The police must be questioning Richard for a reason. Even though I want to believe him, Poirot says I should never rule anyone out.

33

The minutes crawl by the next day at school as all I can do is think about it.

Kate phoned early this morning. She said she didn't think she could cope with identifying the body on her own. Mum was busy with us so Dad said he'd go. I can totally understand her asking, but I do feel sorry for Dad. I know how he felt about it.

Sheralyn's at college and the rest of us are home now, waiting for them to come back, waiting to find out if it's her.

Olivia is not happy as she's had to miss ballet. I don't think Finn's aware enough to know he's missed his swimming lesson too. Mum has decided we should play Pairs to take our minds off things. I say 'we', but Mum and I are playing together and Mum is mostly playing for Finn too. The cards are all laid out face down in rows and we take it in turns to pick two and see if they match. Mum is useless, which is frustrating as I have a good memory and could do much better than Mum if I could only pick the cards myself. Finn is not very interested at first, but he suddenly begins to pick out matching pairs by himself. I've never seen him play a proper game like this. Mum has to restrain him until it's his turn. He is beating Olivia and I can see the tension building in her face. Finn has no interest in winning, of course. I don't think he knows what that means. He's just enjoying matching cards. Olivia will not cope well if she doesn't win, least of all if she is beaten by Finn.

Mum can see this too. She gives a brief lecture, supposedly to everyone, about winning not being everything and how not everyone can win.

Finn gets another pair. Then another. Olivia picks two cards. They match. Phew! She has another turn. This pair doesn't match. She throws those cards down and then kicks the rest of them so that they are all out of position.

'Olivia,' Mum says sternly.

'I'm not playing this poxy game!' Olivia yells and storms out. I hear her feet thudding loudly as she thumps her way upstairs.

Mum sighs. She begins to put the cards in the box,

but then sees that Finn is still playing with them. He turns all the cards face up and proceeds to match them into pairs and line them up. He is trying to make order out of the chaos.

The game had actually distracted me from thinking about Sarah, but now Mum's looking at her watch.

The doorbell rings. I see Mum visibly jump.

Dad has his key – unless he forgot it. I wonder who it is.

I am facing the wrong way. I have to wait for a voice. 'Hiya, any news?' a voice asks softly. Of course – it's Sheralyn. I'm glad she's here.

As Sheralyn comes into the lounge I hear Mum's mobile ring.

'Well?' says Mum.

It must be Dad. I wait – ears straining.

'Oh, goodness,' she says next.

Mum comes into the lounge as Sheralyn is taking off her coat.

I see Mum's smile, but it is a small, sad smile. 'It isn't her,' she tells us. 'The body isn't Sarah.'

Mum flops down in the armchair, still clutching her phone to her ear, speaking into it. 'See you soon, love,' she says.

I'm not sure if I'm crying or if my eye is just watering, but I can feel the wetness running down my cheek.

Finn stands up, looking almost as if he's going to say something. He turns and looks carefully at his lines of pairs. Every card is now matched, but one is slightly out of line. He straightens it and then claps his hands.

Has he heard what Mum said? I'm sure he has.

Sheralyn turns to Mum and then reaches out to give her a hug. Then Mum goes out into the hall, calling up the stairs for Olivia to come down.

'The body isn't Sarah,' I hear Mum tell her.

'Where is she, then?' Olivia asks. 'Where's Sarah? Why doesn't she come back?'

'If it turns out she's gone off somewhere on a whim,' Kate says as we sit round the kitchen table with Mum and Dad. 'I will never forgive her for putting me through that – *never*.'

This sounds weird to me. Surely she should be relieved that the body wasn't Sarah. But she and Dad just looked exhausted when they got back.

Kate starts to cry. 'When they pulled back the

sheet – I was so expecting it to be her and then . . . and then . . .'

'It must have been awful,' says Mum. She looks at Dad. I can't see his face, but his head nods slowly.

Mum goes over to Kate and puts a hand on her shoulder.

'That poor girl,' says Dad. 'The police don't know who she is.'

Dad shudders. Mum goes over and gives him a hug. She kisses him and he hugs her back. I can see the love between them and it warms me inside, like the hot chocolate Mum's just made me that is the perfect temperature. People usually make it too cold as they're so worried about it being too hot!

Dad sits down and sips his coffee.

'Thank you for coming with me,' Kate tells Dad. 'It would have been far worse on my own. I just want to find her. I think she's alive and she's gone off somewhere to sort her head out.'

'I hope you're right,' says Mum.

Soon after Kate leaves, I hear a sudden sobbing sound. It's Mum crying. I think she still blames herself for Sarah going missing.

Poor Mum. I wish I could comfort her and tell her it's not her fault.

And I need her to stay strong. If Mum goes to pieces she might decide she can't look after us any more. Then what would happen?

34

Mum's having a rest upstairs, and Dad and Sheralyn are looking after us. It's evening now and Dan stands awkwardly in the hallway. Dad was wheeling me out of the lounge when the doorbell went, so I'm facing into the hall, wondering what he is doing here.

'I heard about the body they found,' he says. 'Thank God it wasn't her.'

'Yes, Dan, it's a huge relief,' Dad agrees.

'So there's no news at all – no more sightings or anything?' Dan asks.

There's something intense about the way he's asking this.

'No, nothing,' he sighs.

I give an involuntary grunt and Dad glances back towards me. 'If only Jemma could speak,' he says. 'I often wonder what she'd be able to tell us.'

'Yeah – I bet she knows all sorts,' says Dan. He meets my eyes with a stare that makes me shudder.

Dad nods. 'Lorraine took her to a specialist who thinks there might be a way for Jemma to communicate, but we've got to wait to be able to try it.'

'Really?' There's a distinct edge to Dan's voice. His eyes flick over to me again. He watches me and something clouds his expression. His lip twitches as if he is about to say something.

'Is there anything else?' Dad asks.

'No – no, I'll let you get on. I hope you don't mind me popping round. It's just . . . I'm finding it tough, all this, you know.'

'I'm sure you are. We all are,' says Dad, as he sees Dan out.

Dad comes back, sighing and pushes me into the lounge. I realise I must have been holding my breath as it all comes out in a rush. Dan's face when he found out about the specialist. He looked like he was suddenly seeing me differently. Like I might not be so powerless after all. He already wanted me out of the way. If he thinks I could tell his secret, what will he do?

The next morning there is something else for Mum to worry about – me. Maybe it's just exhaustion after everything with Jodi and the body and what Dad told Dan, but my back's aching again and I worry it's another infection. I'm not ill enough to go into hospital, thank goodness, but my temperature's up and I am too ill to go to school.

I think I'd rather be at school to be honest as I don't want to be a strain on Mum, and at least at school there would be other things to think about. Here I can only think about Dan and Sarah and Jodi. I keep imagining Dan waiting outside the house. Working out when he could get me alone. I'm scared of Dan and I'm scared I will never see Sarah or Jodi again.

I'm in bed. Mum checks me every ten minutes and takes my temperature. If it gets too high I will have to go to hospital. Every bit of my body aches.

'I'm so sorry, Jemma,' Mum sighs. 'Life's the pits at the moment, isn't it?'

She's right. I feel so low – the lowest I can remember feeling. There's no point to anything any more. I used to be content to watch, but now I don't like anything I'm seeing. Not being able to tell what I know is unbearable. I can do nothing – and Dan is running around free. I'm a complete waste of space. I'm a burden to everyone. I can't tell anyone about

Dan. I couldn't protect Sarah. My own sister wanted to know me until she actually saw me and then she changed her mind. What is the point of me being alive?

I feel so achy, so weak. They'll have to send me to the hospital soon.

Then I have a thought – a crazy thought. That would be Dan's chance, wouldn't it? That was how he got me on my own before. If Dan killed me and got caught, then they'd work it all out.

I feel a weird elation and my heartbeat races. Maybe all these thoughts have finally sent me mad.

I'm getting hot and sticky. Mum takes my temperature again. She tuts. 'It's too high, Jemma. This is no good. I'm going to call the hospital.'

On this trip to hospital I am aware of everything – every corner turned, every bump in the road. I don't want to live any more. Not having a sister was OK. Having one but not seeing her is horrible. It was bad enough not being able to communicate, but having something I desperately need to say and not being able to say it is too much to bear.

*

I am woken by a cough – a man's cough. It's not Dad. I'd recognise Dad's cough. I'm in hospital – I can smell the disinfectant. There's a man standing close to me. Is it Dan? Has he come already? I can't see. I am facing the wrong way for a start, but I can't see anyway. I try to focus, but my vision is blurry.

Right now I want Mum. *I want Mum!* A hand squeezes mine. It is a warm, soft hand.

'It's OK, Jemma. I'm here,' Mum says gently.

'Ah, Jemma, you're awake,' comes a man's voice from the other side of the bed. He has a strong accent. It's definitely not Dan.

'I'm Doctor Sargent,' the voice continues. He speaks slowly and loudly, as if I might not understand.

Mum turns my head so that I can see a blurry white coat. The doctor is leaning over me. 'You're rather poorly,' he continues, like I don't know that, 'and we've had to give you some medicine. Don't worry if your vision is a bit fuzzy. It's a side effect, but it should settle down.'

I am relieved to have an explanation for the blurriness.

Mum stays a long time and I don't know how long she's been here already. I sleep and wake and sleep and wake and she's still here. Now I wake and think she's gone as I can't feel her hand, but I hear a snorting sound and then another. Mum's hand has slipped from mine and she's actually asleep. She's snoring. Poor Mum. This is too much for her.

Dad comes eventually and takes over. Then Sheralyn for a bit. They rotate. I mainly sleep. I dream about Dan.

'*If I were you, I'd top myself. Listen, if you ever want a bit of help, I could –*'

In my dream I am able to nod and then he is holding a pillow. It is coming down towards my face. I think, *This is it. This is the end.*

35

I've been here overnight. I know I will have to wait for Dan to find out I'm here, but I'm sure it won't take him long. Someone else comes – someone I'm not expecting.

It's Paula.

'This is so kind of you,' Mum tells her. 'I wouldn't leave Jemma with someone she doesn't know – but you know Paula well enough, don't you?' Mum looks at me and squeezes my hand. 'It's just for a bit. I have to go up to Olivia's school.'

I wonder briefly what's happened with Olivia. Has she hit someone else? Then my thoughts turn to Paula. My vision is clear again now, thank goodness. Paula's chunky knit jumper does not disguise how thin she's getting. Her cheekbones are almost poking out of her face and her hands look so bony there is barely any flesh on them. I hope she's not going to hold my hand. She shifts from one foot to another anxiously.

It's taken her courage to offer to do this and I admire her for that, but I'm not sure I want her here. Actually, I'm sure I don't.

'It's no bother at all,' Paula tells Mum. 'You've been so kind to us – I'm glad to be able to do something for you.'

'I've brought a book, if you fancy reading it to her,' Mum tells Paula.

Paula nods.

Then Mum has gone.

Paula picks up the book and turns it over. I realise at once that she's not going to want to read it. It's not the vampire romance, though I'm not sure Paula would like that much either. It's a murder mystery! I hope she doesn't think Mum is too insensitive for suggesting it. Paula sighs and puts it down.

'Your mum says you understand everything so I'm sure you do. I wish they'd catch Ryan's killer. I want to know what happened and why, and I want whoever did it locked up. Is that too much to ask, Jemma?'

She sounds like she's caught in a loop – like she's said the words so many times. I wish I could speak to her. I could change things.

'Between you and me there's something I haven't

told the police, Jemma – and I don't know what to do,' she continues, leaning forwards and speaking quietly.

I had slightly lost concentration as she rambled on, but now I am alert.

'Before it happened,' Paula tells me, 'Ryan asked me to hide some stuff for him. I know I shouldn't have – I should've at least asked what was going on, but he clearly didn't want to tell me. I know I was stupid, but I did what he asked. I wanted to keep him out of trouble.'

She pauses and I want to ask, 'What stuff?'

She edges even closer and her voice is lower, almost a whisper. 'It was jewellery, Jemma – diamond rings, gold necklaces . . . and I think Ryan might have stolen it,' she says. 'I didn't want the police to know he was a thief – they already know he was a drug user. They might have written him off – not bothered to look for his killer. So I hid the things. I'm sure I shouldn't have done, but I promised him and I hid them – and when the police came looking for clues I didn't tell them. I couldn't cope with Graeme finding out what I'd done – and I didn't want to get myself in trouble too.'

I watch Paula – her eyes look straight through me like I'm not even here and she's constantly rubbing her fingers together as she talks. It reminds me of Dan when Mum said the police were looking for him. It looks as if this guilt has been eating her up.

'It didn't occur to me at the time – but now I'm worried that the stuff belonged to the person who killed Ryan. What do you think, Jemma? I wish you could tell me – I bet you could work it out better than me.'

Maybe I *could* work it out. I need to think . . .

'The thing is, I don't know what to do now,' Paula continues, sighing. 'Should I go to the police and tell them? I'm scared I might get arrested for withholding evidence. I could say I only just found them . . . but the police did such a thorough search they might not believe me. How will Graeme cope if I get banged up in prison? That's why I haven't even told him.'

Paula suddenly sits up straighter. 'I'm sorry, Jemma. I shouldn't be talking to you about this, should I? It's rotten of me. You're ill – you don't want to hear about Ryan – especially when you have Sarah to worry about too. Let's talk about something else.'

But she clearly can't think of anything. She glances briefly at the book, but I can see she can't face picking it up. So we sit silently and she twiddles her thumbs.

I think about Ryan. I didn't know him well, but it sounds likely that he did steal the things Paula found. Why would someone kill him for that, though? Maybe he owed money for the drugs, and he stole the things intending to sell them. Could there be any link with Dan and Sarah? Maybe Ryan stole the jewellery from Dan and that's why Dan killed him. Then Sarah found out and he had to kill her too. The black jacket comes into my head. Could Graeme have been involved? Could he have found the jewellery and confronted Ryan? Or could Graeme have stolen them and Ryan found out? Then I remember Dan's face when Dad said I might be able to communicate.

Paula's phone beeps and she pulls it from her bag in relief and continues to look at it, touching different areas of the screen for what feels like a long time.

36

Sheralyn takes over from Paula, and Mum comes back after lunch. I'm not feeling much better. I feel so, so tired.

Mum smiles as she sits down and I notice she has big bags under her eyes. I want her here – but I also wish she could go home and get some sleep.

'I'm sorry I couldn't be here,' says Mum. 'I hope you were OK with Paula. Olivia's getting herself into all sorts of trouble at school.' Mum is scrabbling around in her bag as she speaks. 'I've persuaded them to give her another chance, but I'm not sure she'll be able to stay there if she keeps kicking off. More parents have been complaining.'

Mum's bag is bulging. An old shopping list, a pen and a lipstick fly out and she hastily retrieves them from the floor.

I hope Olivia isn't going to get herself chucked out of her school. I wonder what she did. I wish I could tell Mum what Olivia told me about Dylan.

'Here it is,' Mum says finally.

It's a letter. I see straight away that it is Jodi's writing on the front. My heart starts thudding and my stomach churns. I don't know what to expect or how to feel. Jodi has written – but what has she said?

'I hope you don't mind that I opened it first,' Mum says. 'I didn't want to bring it if it was going to upset you. Not with you being so ill.'

Mum pulls the letter out of the envelope.

'Dear Jemma,

'It's really hard to write this, but I hate thinking how upset you must be with me. I'll understand if you hate me and never want to see me again. I want you to know, though, that's not how I feel about you.

'I want to explain what happened – or try to at least. I think I had a kind of image of you in my head and I guess you didn't look anything like I was expecting. I know your mum sent a photo, but until I saw you I had no idea how much you looked like me. I know we're twins, but I just wasn't expecting it for some reason. You must have seen that too – we are so alike!

'You also – this sounds really bad, but I want to be honest

– you look much more disabled than I expected. I knew you were in a wheelchair and that you can't speak, but it was a shock to see you.'

I flinch as Mum reads this. She's referring to the strange shape of my head, my gaping mouth. I don't want to be a shock to look at, but there's not much I can do about that.

Mum continues.

'I thought I'd just be able to start talking – I had so much I wanted to say I wasn't worried about you not talking back. I'm quite a blabbermouth usually! No one else can get a word in. So I thought I would be OK.

'I froze up, Jemma, and everything I wanted to say went out of my head. I felt so stupid standing there unable to speak. I don't know where the tears came from, but once I started I couldn't stop and I felt even worse so I had to just get out of there.

'I want you to know that I do want to try again. You are my sister and I want to know you and for you to know me.

'Please, please forgive me and let's start over – please!

'Love, Jodi x x x.'

My sister still wants to know me.

The warm feeling spreads through my body – I can even feel it in my legs and arms and I can't feel much there usually.

'I can see that's brought some colour back to your face!' Mum exclaims. She strokes my cheek gently and touches my brow. 'Yes, it's not fever – just a healthy glow.'

'When can I see her again?' I want to ask Mum.

She doesn't tell me, but I will forgive her for that because I am so happy about the letter. I wish I could hold it, smell it, keep it. I don't want Mum to fold it and put it in her bag. I wish she'd stick it on the wall beside my bed so I can look at it and read it over and over.

I try to remember the words, as Mum puts her bag back on the floor.

You are my sister and I want to know you.

That is all I need. I say it over and over in my head. From her to me and me to her. I feel it. I live it. I don't want to die. I don't want Dan to kill me any more, even if it helps the police catch him.

I feel the strength returning to my body all day. I want to see Jodi. I need to get well.

37

Mum calls Jodi and arranges for us to meet her on Sunday. It's only two days to wait, but once I'm home all I can think about is Sarah. Her absence is like a wide open window through which a cold breeze constantly blows. I cannot feel warm and safe and happy – even knowing I will soon meet my sister again. What has happened to Sarah?

Mum still looks stressed out – and worse, she says Sheralyn has a bad cold and won't be able to help for a few days.

After dinner Finn and Olivia go upstairs. Dad's not back as he has a late meeting at work. Mum pushes me out of the kitchen, saying she'll put the telly on for me while she gets them ready for bed. As we reach the living room, the phone rings.

'Back in a tick,' she tells me, sighing – and rushes off without even putting the light on, let alone the telly. I expect her to pick up the phone in the hallway and bring it back in here, but she must have taken it into the kitchen as her voice gets more distant.

She must be speaking quietly. I can't hear what she's saying or work out who she's talking to. I hear the phone click, but it rings again almost immediately. I only hear 'yes', 'no' and 'I should think so'. Then 'I'll let you know if I hear anything'.

I can't believe Mum has left me here in the dark. I'm trying to hear her, but I get a sudden sense of someone behind me. I can hear breathing – loud breathing – as if someone is panting by the living-room door. My heart races. I'm not imagining it. Someone's here.

Has Dan got in? Was he waiting outside? He didn't come to the hospital, but he's here now! He's used Sarah's key to get in. He could have been in the house for hours – just waiting for the right moment.

The breathing is coming nearer.

'Mum!' I want to scream. 'Get off the phone! Get in here now!'

He is right behind me. I feel my wheelchair jolt. What is he going to do?

My chair jolts again. The breathing is still close

– but . . . what's happened? The sound of breathing is right underneath me – under my chair!

There is a *bang, bang* against the right wheel. I suddenly realise – it's Finn! Finn is under my chair, panting and banging his head against one of the wheels.

I try to steady my breathing. This whole Sarah thing must be affecting him badly. He's under my chair – wanting me to keep him safe, to make everything OK. He is trying to tell me how bad he feels. I wish I could do something – make everything better. I wish I could bring Sarah back.

At last I hear Mum's footsteps. But she doesn't appear. I hear her feet *thump, thump* up the stairs. She thinks Finn's up there. She's forgotten about me altogether.

She's gone up. Finn's breathing has slowed down, but I can still hear it. Mum's feet are soon on the stairs again because she hasn't found Finn.

'Finn! Finn, love! Are you down here?'

She approaches the living room and turns the light on. She gasps.

'Jemma!' As she comes round in front of me, I am shocked to see she is sobbing. Tears are rolling down her cheeks. 'I've left you here in the dark! I completely forgot! I'm so sorry, I'm so sorry, Jemma. I'm losing it. And I can't find Finn.'

She collapses on to the sofa, crying. I can't bear to see Mum like this. If Mum falls apart social services will take us all away. It's a terrifying thought. She has to get it together. She mustn't let that happen!

At that moment I hear Dad's key in the door.

He hears her sobbing and is by her side in seconds. 'What's happened?' Dad says softly. 'Have they found her?'

'No, no – it's not Sarah, it's Jemma. I forgot her,' Mum sobs. 'I left her in the dark when the phone rang. I left her in the dark for about twenty minutes! And I can't find Finn!'

Dad sees him straight away. 'That's easy, love – look, he's under Jemma's chair!'

'My God,' Mum exclaims. 'Finn, what are you doing there?'

Finn doesn't come out.

'If Sheralyn can't help, we've got to get the agency to send another carer,' Dad says.

'Other families have to get by without carers,' says Mum.

'Yes,' says Dad, 'but we wouldn't have taken on

the other two if we didn't have that help with Jemma.'

'I didn't want to get someone else – Sarah . . . I thought she'd be back,' says Mum, wiping her eyes with her sleeve.

'I'm sure she will,' says Dad, though he doesn't sound convincing, 'but in the meantime we need someone.'

38

Dad has ordered Mum to take it easy and the agency carer arrives after breakfast. She is smiley and bubbly although her voice is a little loud.

'Hey, this must be Jemma!' she says.

'This is Rosie,' Mum tells me.

'I can see we both like purple!' Rosie says, beaming at me. She points to my cardigan and her purple top. 'We're going to get on just fine!'

Sarah chose that purple cardigan for me. I feel a pang.

Mum smiles at Rosie. 'That's great. I'm so glad you could come so quickly,' she says. 'Let me tell you a bit about Jemma.'

'It's OK,' says Rosie. 'The agency filled me in. And I have lots of experience. You can leave us to get to know each other.'

'Good,' says Mum. 'Just call me if there's anything you need.'

There's an awkward silence as Mum heads off upstairs.

'I hear you like books,' Rosie says. 'I thought I could read to you, OK?'

I am relieved, although she's not quite speaking like a normal person.

She goes to her big purple rucksack, which is on the sofa. 'I always carry books with me!' she says. 'Hang on a tick – let me see what you might like.'

I wish she'd just get the book that's on my bedside cabinet, the one Mum's reading to me.

'Hey, this is a great one!' says Rosie. The sing-song enthusiasm in her voice is already getting to me, but I will give her a chance. I look to see what book she's holding. The size of it and the brightly coloured cover make me swallow hard. It's a fairy-tale picture book. *The Little Mermaid*.

This has to be a joke. No – she's wheeling me close to the sofa so she can sit beside me.

'I know you'll want to see the pictures!' she tells me, holding the book so it rests on my lap.

No one has told her I have a brain. She also hasn't thought to ask. I hope Mum will look in soon to check how she's getting on and put her right.

Mum doesn't come. I have to endure *The Little Mermaid* read in a patronising voice with every picture pointed out. 'Look there's the mermaid! 'Look there's a crab!' I don't even like the story of *The Little Mermaid*.

Finally it's over. 'Do you like music?' Rosie asks me. 'I bet you do! I've brought some with me, specially.'

This sounds encouraging – though if it is Glowlight I won't be able to bear it.

She pulls out her phone and swipes a few times. 'Here we go!' I listen as the music begins. It's a baby song – 'The Wheels on the Bus'. This is utter humiliation. I am not a toddler in a teenage body, I am an actual teenager. I am fourteen!

She begins to wheel me round in dance-like movements, jerking me uncomfortably and singing along.

This is a nightmare.

Then I hear a laugh. It is a raucous, jeering kind of laugh. As I am spun round I see Olivia standing in the doorway, laughing hysterically. The humiliation can't get any worse.

'Hey, do you want to join us?' Rosie asks her. 'We're having a great time here!'

'You might be,' says Olivia. 'I don't think SHE is.'

'No?' Rosie stops still. She turns me round to face her and looks at me closely. 'It's hard to tell,' she admits.

'She's not stupid,' Olivia says.

'Of course not,' says Rosie. 'But she –'

'She's fourteen. She likes teenager stuff – not baby stuff.'

'Thank you, Olivia!' I want to shout.

'Are you sure?' Rosie asks. 'I thought bright colours and simple rhymes would be the right thing. I mean, how do you know what she likes or what she's thinking when she can't speak?'

'I just know,' says Olivia. 'I know loads of stuff, actually. I like teenage stuff too. I nearly am a teenager.'

'Really?' Rosie is looking more and more uncomfortable. 'So how old are you?'

'Nine,' Olivia says, 'but I'll be a teenager in only four years. I know loads of things that teenagers know – loads.'

'OK,' says Rosie. 'So what do you suggest we do? What would you and Jemma – you teenagers – like to do now?

Olivia looks thoughtful. I wonder what she's going to come up with.

'Watch telly?' she says. 'We can watch *Fuzz Heads*. There's this really hot boy on it.'

'Hot boy?' Rosie repeats, wide-eyed. 'I'm not sure . . .'

'Mum lets me watch it. Even Finn watches it and he's six,' says Olivia.

'I'm not sure your mum will be happy to pay me to sit and watch TV,' Rosie says doubtfully.

'I'm sure she will,' says Olivia. 'I promise you.'

I don't like *Fuzz Heads*, but I am begging Rosie to agree.

'OK – just for a few minutes,' Rosie says.

'Yay!' says Olivia, plonking herself on the sofa.

When Mum comes down with Finn I can see from her expression that she is not pleased we are watching TV.

'I read to Jemma and played her some music,' Rosie assures Mum.

'Yeah – she put on nursery rhymes!' says Olivia.

'Nursery rhymes?' Mum exclaims. 'Why would you do that?'

'I didn't know . . .' Rosie says. 'I thought –'

'No, you didn't think!' Mum yells.

I am shocked to hear Mum raise her voice like this. It is so unlike her.

'You have to leave. Now,' Mum tells her, pointing to the door. 'Jemma is an intelligent young woman and I cannot imagine how she felt. This is outrageous.'

'I'm so, so sorry,' Rosie says, her sing-song voice gone and a feeble whisper coming out. 'I really didn't mean –'

'Just go,' says Mum.

Although I am not keen on Rosie I actually feel sorry for her in that moment – and surprised at Mum reacting so strongly. I'd have expected Mum to be cross and to explain, but I thought she'd give Rosie a second chance.

Once Rosie's gone I see Mum grab a bar of chocolate from between two books on the shelf and wolf the lot.

After dinner there's a call from Kate. Dad answers, and he looks shocked when he comes back into the kitchen.

'They arrested Richard yesterday,' Dad tells us. 'They've been questioning him and they've applied for permission to hold him for longer.'

'*Richard*?' Mum says. 'He seemed so nice and so genuinely upset when we told him she was missing.'

'He was a bit of a mess, if you ask me,' said Dad. 'I'm still surprised, though.'

The police have the wrong man! I am sure of it. And while they're busy questioning Richard they won't be thinking about Dan.

39

Last night I dreamed that Sarah came back – walked through the door as if nothing had happened. She said she'd lost her memory and she had no idea where she'd been for the last few weeks. She put me to bed as usual and turned me in the night. She smiled like she always did and I knew that everything was going to go back to normal. Everything was going to be OK.

I woke this morning and had that sinking feeling I always get now when I realise Sarah is still missing. I don't think everything is ever going to be normal again. Then I remember that today is not a normal day – not even a 'normal without Sarah' day. Today I am meeting Jodi. I'm trying to wipe that first meeting out of my mind and just think about her last letter. The same thing can't happen again – I'm sure. This time we are meeting in a café. My social worker, Beth, and Donna, the social worker who came to support Jodi last time, are going to be there too.

The waiting was so awful last time that Mum's decided we should be a few minutes late in the hope that Jodi will already be there. Either that or we are just running late anyway!

Mum manoeuvres my wheelchair into the café. It's big inside at least and not busy. I see Jodi with Donna and Beth, at a spacious table in the corner. She's here. My tummy wobbles. Donna sees us and jumps up to move chairs so I can get near to the table.

'Hi, Jemma. Come and join us. Come and meet Jodi properly,' she says.

Jodi gives me a quick smile and then turns away awkwardly. She looks stiff and terrified. I wonder if she is going to run off again.

Everyone says hello. Beth comes and hugs me – I haven't seen her for a while. She looks from me to Jodi and smiles, talking in her low, soothing voice. 'I feel quite emotional seeing you together. You can certainly tell that you're twins! I can imagine what a big deal this must be for both of you.'

'I'm so glad you decided to come,' Mum says to Jodi.

'It was hard.' Jodi nods. 'I was just . . . overwhelmed.'

She looks quickly at me and back to Mum. 'I hope she doesn't mind me saying that?'

I wish so much that I could smile at her, reassure her, tell her it's fine. It's enough that she's here.

'Don't worry so much,' Donna tells her. 'You'll be fine.'

'I don't know what to say,' Jodi continues, giving me another brief, awkward glance. She shuffles anxiously on her chair. 'Like last time – I could think of loads to talk about before I got here, but now I am, it feels so much harder . . .'

'You're getting yourself worked up,' says Donna. 'Don't upset yourself. Just start talking.'

Jodi's face crumples. She looks even more like me for a moment. She's going to bottle it. I can see it in her eyes. She's going to get up and leave.

'Why don't you come closer and hold Jemma's hand?' Beth suggests. 'I think Jemma would love that – and you don't need to talk at all unless you want to.'

Jodi's shoulders seem to relax. She smiles gratefully at Beth, stands up and moves her chair closer to mine.

She looks at me, her eyes still frightened, but there is warmth in them. I can see it. I can feel it.

'I'd like to hold your hand, Jemma,' she tells me.

She touches and then she squeezes gently. Her hand is soft and smooth and warm. It feels a similar size to mine, although mine is bony and clenched.

I feel a weird sense of connectedness – it is different from anyone else who has ever held my hand. This is my sister – my twin.

A waitress comes and takes our order for drinks. Jodi orders a smoothie and Mum orders me an apple juice, asking for a straw.

Jodi says nothing, but I don't mind. Mum was right. I want her to talk at some point – I want to know all about her – but right now it is enough that my sister is holding my hand.

40

'What hobbies do you have?' Beth prompts Jodi. 'Maybe you could tell Jemma about them.'

I'm so glad Beth's here. Donna is nice, but Beth's calmness and suggestions are definitely helping.

'Oh . . . well . . .' says Jodi, 'I told Jemma some stuff already in my letters . . . I like reading.' She starts off looking at Beth and then at Mum. 'My favourite authors are John Green and Suzanne Collins. I've just been reading *Paper Towns*. It's about a guy who goes on a road trip to find a girl. It's brilliant.'

'We read to Jemma a lot,' Mum tells Jodi. 'We'll have to look out for that book.'

'I can lend it to you,' says Jodi.

'That would be lovely,' says Mum. 'Maybe you could even read some to Jemma, yourself?'

Jodi's face lights up. 'Yes – I'd love to!'

I like the sound of the book. It's not the kind of

thing I usually listen to, but I'd love Jodi to read it to me.

'I'm quite sporty too,' Jodi continues. She's still talking mainly to Mum, but I can forgive her because at least she is talking now.

'I play hockey for the county. Maybe you could bring Jemma and come and watch one day?'

I know nothing about hockey, but watching Jodi play would be really cool. If I wasn't disabled would I have been sporty too? It's not something I've ever thought about.

'That's great,' says Mum. 'I'm sure Jemma would love to.'

The waitress comes at that moment with our drinks.

'Do you want to give Jemma her drink?' Mum asks Jodi.

Jodi frowns. 'No . . . I . . . I don't know. I don't want to spill it down her or something . . .'

'Don't worry. Just watch me,' Mum tells her.

Jodi lets go of my hand and Mum comes closer, pushing the straw carefully into my mouth.

'I could hold the glass now, if you like?' says Jodi. Mum passes it to her.

Jodi's face is close, very close to mine. I like that

she's giving me my drink, the way she's focusing every ounce of her attention on me.

Mum shifts her chair a little further away and begins to chat to Beth and Donna.

'I'll tell you something else I like,' Jodi says, putting my glass down carefully on the table. She clasps my hand in hers and carries on. 'Do you want to know my favourite band?'

For the first time she is talking directly to me and not partly through Mum.

'I totally love Glowlight,' she continues. 'Have you heard of them?'

My heart almost stops beating. She loves Glowlight – just like me. And Sarah – poor Sarah. I wish I could speak – I wish I could tell her all about the concert, about Sarah going missing.

'I wanted to go to their last concert a few weeks back, but I couldn't get tickets. I'd love to see them live one day.'

She is still talking – now she's started she can't stop. She's telling me about other bands she likes, some I've heard of and some I haven't – but I am thinking only of Glowlight. I can hear their lyrics in my head.

'Shall I tell you more about me?' she says.

'Yes!' I want to say.

'So, I was adopted when I was eight months old, but I've always known. Maybe you've been wondering why my mum and dad didn't adopt you too?' Jodi says anxiously.

'Don't worry, that's pretty obvious,' I want to tell her.

'I think it's because we had different needs. That's right, isn't it, Donna?'

'Sorry – what?' Donna says. She's been chatting to the others and not listening in, which pleases me.

Jodi repeats her question.

'Yes, Jemma. Jodi's parents never met you. You went to separate foster homes as your needs were very specialised. People who want to take in children who need special care like you need special skills – like your mum.' She smiles at Mum. 'You both have parents who love you – that's what matters, isn't it?'

I wish we had been able to stay together, though I realise what she's getting at. If we had, no one would have adopted both of us. At least on her own, Jodi had a good chance. And Mum and Dad are long-term foster parents so it's not really different from being adopted. I couldn't ask for better parents than them.

'I think it's awful that we were split up,' Jodi says to me. 'My mum said the social worker told them they should tell me about you, but they decided not to. She said she realises now they did the wrong thing.

'Anyway, I bet there's loads you want to ask me and tell me! I can't imagine how frustrating it must be not being able to speak. I think I'd go crazy. I mean – I'm not saying you're crazy, you know that – don't you? I just mean it must be hard. I hope they get something sorted for you soon.'

She's right. I am going crazy inside – and she doesn't know half of what I need to say.

Mum stands up and comes nearer. 'How's it going?' she asks.

'Great,' says Jodi. 'Thank you so much for giving me another chance.' Jodi is reaching into her bag. She pulls out her phone. 'Can you take a picture of us?'

'What a lovely idea!' says Mum. 'I'm sure Jemma would like one too. I'll take one with my phone.'

Jodi pulls her chair round beside mine, clutching my hand. Mum clicks away. I am delighted. I will have a photo of me and Jodi. I hope Mum will put it by my bed. I'm sure she will.

*

It's horrible saying goodbye to Jodi and I want them to arrange another day to meet, but Jodi says we will and I believe her. And there is another nice surprise when I get home. Sheralyn's back. She's feeling better, thank goodness, and Mum is still looking so tired. Sheralyn isn't Sarah – but she's a great improvement on Rosie.

Sheralyn reads to me. She has a nice reading voice, but she's not as good as Sarah. Sarah gave each character a different voice and she read with such expression I used to wonder if she'd ever tried acting. I think she'd have been good.

Mum printed the photo of Jodi and me, and now it is by my bed. I thought it might bother me that Jodi is beautiful and I am not, but when I look at the picture all I see is the likeness. She is what I was meant to be – what I really am inside. Seeing her I feel as if I am that beautiful. It makes me feel stronger. It's hard to explain, but I never imagined before that even if I wasn't disabled that I would have looked so lovely. Now I can imagine it and instead of feeling sad that I am not the same as her, I feel happy. I almost look as if I am smiling in the picture and Jodi is definitely smiling.

Olivia comes to look at it.

'I wish I had a sister,' she says.

I feel sorry for her. I want to say, 'But I'm your sister, Olivia. We're a family – you, me, Finn, Mum and Dad.'

Olivia picks up the picture and holds it close to her eyes. I want her to put it back. I feel protective of it and I'm scared she's going to scrunch it or even tear it.

Sheralyn comes in.

'Maybe I've got a sister too, like Jemma,' Olivia says.

'Maybe,' says Sheralyn. She sounds doubtful.

'Can you find out?' Olivia demands. 'I want to know.'

'I'll ask your mum,' says Sheralyn, 'but I think someone would have told you if you have a sister.'

Olivia puts the photo down on my bedside cabinet – but she's laid it down flat so I can't see it. I panic. I feel an urgent need to see it, to keep it visible – as if Jodi might cease to exist or cease to be my sister if I can't see the picture of the two of us. I might wake and find it was all a dream. Sheralyn is my lifesaver – she notices and stands it up for me.

'Come on, Olivia – off to bed now,' says Sheralyn.

41

I've been on a high since meeting Jodi. I enjoyed swimming at school yesterday, especially as the water was warmer than last week. Then in the changing rooms I overheard my teacher asking Sheralyn if there was any news about my carer and I felt pangs of guilt. How can I even be happy for a second when Sarah is still missing? Last night I heard Dad tell Mum that Richard's been released and I'm relieved about that, though Kate still thinks he did it. She thinks they just didn't have enough evidence to charge him. Everyone's so focused on Richard now they're missing the truth. They're not thinking about Dan.

Today Sheralyn's gone to college. I'm ready for school, but my transport hasn't turned up. Mum phones and discovers the minibus has broken down.

Finn's transport came and luckily Dad was still here so he's taken Olivia. Mum says she'll take me to school herself.

She is pushing me out of the front door when the phone rings inside. She sighs, pulling me back a little and then pushing me forward. I can't see her face, of course, but I can tell she's not sure whether to take the call or not.

She pulls me jerkily back inside and I hear her footsteps down the hall – running to pick up the phone.

'Oh!' Mum sounds like she's walking towards the front door. There is real surprise in her voice – so much so that I actually wonder for an instant if it is Sarah herself calling.

'I wasn't expecting to hear from you. We got your letter, of course, but July – it is so far away . . .'

Professor Spalding! Why is he phoning?

'Really?' I hear Mum say. 'Is he? When would that be?' There's a long pause. It seems to go on forever. Then finally she says, 'Yes, I'm sure that would be fine.' And there's silence again, but I can hear that she's taking notes.

A few minutes later Mum is back, pushing me out of the door again.

'Well, it's good I took that call, Jemma,' she says. 'The researcher from Israel who has created the sniffing technology decided at short notice to come to a conference in England this week and Professor Spalding says he wants to meet you.'

What? I can't believe this. He's actually here?

'Mr Katz would like to try his sniffing equipment with you. He wants us to meet him tomorrow!'

The waiting room at the National Hospital for Neurology and Neurosurgery is big and busy. Hospitals to me always mean long waits. Mum gets a coffee from the machine so she is clearly thinking the same.

'I don't want you to get your hopes up too high, Jemma,' Mum says quietly. 'If this doesn't work, don't worry – we'll keep trying until we find a way. Technology is developing and changing so fast.'

From a look at her face, I can see the hope in her eyes. I heard the high-pitched excitement in her voice when she came off the phone yesterday. She does believe it – I'm sure she does. But do I? What if I can't do it – or I can't master it quickly enough and they decide it won't work? Will they give me a chance to practise?

Nurses with lists have been calling people, but then I see a man in a suit with dark hair, tanned skin and a beard come into the waiting room and look around.

He spots me. I see his eyes stop and his bushy eyebrows go up. He walks confidently towards us.

'Jemma Shaw?' he asks, looking at me and then Mum. He has a strong accent and a serious expression. I wish he'd smile. Maybe he doesn't think this will work either.

Mum stands up quickly and introduces us.

'Alon Katz,' the man says, nodding at each of us and then holding his hand out to Mum. 'Please follow me,' he tells us.

He heads off through the double doors and along a corridor, into a small room.

'I am sorry it is a little tight for space in here,' he says as Mum awkwardly parks me between a chair and a desk.

Mum sits down on the chair beside me and squeezes my hand as Mr Katz picks up glasses from the desk and puts them on. In front of him is what looks like a thin plastic tube with some bits sticking out of it.

'This is it,' he tells us. 'This is the sniff controller. It is still in the research phase, you understand. We have had success using this equipment with patients suffering paralysis following accidents, even with some who were thought to be in a vegetative state. We have not tried it though on someone with cerebral palsy, and my colleague Professor Spalding thought you would be an interesting case for me.'

I can't see Mum's face, but I wonder if she is as surprised as I am. I expected some complicated machine or something – not just a plastic tube.

'We attach this with these sensors just inside the nostril,' he explains. 'The other end can be attached to whatever a person is trying to control – a computer, a communication device, even movement of a wheelchair.'

'Really?' says Mum. 'It looks so . . . simple.'

I see what I am sure is a slight smile behind the beard of Mr Katz.

'First, I will check your ability to control your sniffs,' Mr Katz says, approaching me. He has the tube in his hand. 'This won't hurt –' he tells me – 'but it may feel a little odd at first, having something in your nose. The sensor is only tiny, though.'

He leans very close into my face. I can feel his breath, hot against my cheeks. One hand is on my chin, holding my head steady. I wish my head would stop pulling away from him. He might think I'm objecting, but it's just my body not behaving. I want to try this. I really do.

He stands back. My nose does feel strange – a bit tickly. I hope I don't sneeze the thing out.

'We will attach it to this computer,' says Mr Katz, fiddling with the other end of the tube. 'Now you see this on the screen? This line here will move when you sniff. Try a small sniff, Jemma – in through your nose.'

Oh brilliant. I feel so nervous I think I've forgotten how to sniff!

'In through your nose,' he repeats gently.

I must – I must. I can do it – he must see I can do it. I sniff. The green line bounces on the screen. I did it! I made that happen. I do it again – even though he hasn't told me to. I want to see the line move.

'Good . . . good,' he says slowly. 'Now try a bigger sniff.'

I do it – and straight away the line soars up the screen.

'There.' He grins – and I think this is the moment he is sure. The little sniffs might have been accidental, but this time he knows it is for real.

'Another big one, please,' he asks.

The line soars again.

'Now a small one.'

This is easy. I can do this – I really can. I can make things happen!

I practise this a bit more and then Mr Katz presses a few keys on the keyboard. The screen with the line disappears. I feel disappointed. I could have kept doing that all day. I was making the line move. I was doing it myself. I don't want to stop now.

There is something else on the screen.

'On this screen you will see two words,' he tells me. '*YES* on one side on the green background and *NO* on the other side on the red.'

He points to the words. I want to say, 'I can read – I don't need you to point,' but I try to stay calm.

'You will see the cursor here is constantly moving from one word to the other, every few seconds? I will ask you a question. You will sniff when the cursor is on the answer you wish to give. OK? Big sniff when the cursor is where you want it.'

This is my chance to communicate. This is it! What is he going to ask me?

'Do I have a beard?'

What?

It takes me a moment to take his question in. He is

very still. So is Mum. I can hear them both breathing. I must stay calm. I can do this. I already know I can.

I wait for the cursor to move. I do a big sniff.

'YES,' says a loud woman's voice.

I lurch inside. I didn't expect the computer to actually speak the word. The *YES* on the green side of screen is flashing too. But it is the voice that I can't get over.

'Good. Let's try another one. Is the wall in this room red?

The cursor is on *NO*. I am worried it will move to yes before I manage to sniff. I sniff quickly.

'NO,' says the voice.

I am ready for it this time, but still enthralled to hear it.

I have a voice.

42

Mr Katz asks a few more questions – crazy questions like 'Is the sky blue?' and 'Do dogs have six legs?' Then he asks, 'Do you like the sniff controller?'

I do a big sniff for 'YES'. Then two more. 'YES. YES.'

Mr Katz smiles a proper smile, then.

He turns to Mum. 'Would you like to ask something of Jemma?'

'Gosh,' says Mum, coming round to face me. 'There are so many things I want to ask, I can't think . . .'

Mum hesitates.

'Meeting Jodi . . .' she says finally. 'Are you glad you met her? Please be honest, Jemma.'

'YES,' I sniff.

Mum stares at me, her eyes open wide as she takes in the fact that she's asked me a question and I have answered it. I can't quite believe it either.

Her lip quivers and she rubs her eye. Her mouth

opens and then shuts again. Then she smiles. 'Good, I'm so relieved,' she says. 'I hoped so much that it was the right thing.'

'YES,' I sniff.

I wish the voice of my 'yes' had as much cnthusiasm as I feel. I sniff 'YES' and 'YES' again just be clear.

'Now let's try a letter board,' says Mr Katz. 'I understand from Professor Spalding that you can read, Jemma, but don't worry too much about correct spellings.'

Things are moving fast. Am I ready for a letter board?

I watch as a screen with three panels appears. One is the alphabet spread across four rows. The next is numbers. The third panel is an empty green block. Underneath these three is a wide white block. *YES* and *NO* was one thing, but how can I possibly control this?

'This is very basic software that you can use to spell out words,' Mr Katz explains. 'The sniff controller can be linked to any communication software on a computer or tablet, so if this works, a speech therapist can help to identify the best software for you.'

Mr Katz points at the screen. 'As with the *YES* and *NO* screen, the cursor moves between the blocks, as you see. If you want a letter, give a big sniff when you reach the letter block. The cursor will then move from row to row. Give a small sniff when it reaches the row you want. The cursor will then move along that row and you can select a letter with another small sniff. What you type will appear in the white box below. In the green box you will see predictive text, but don't concern yourself with that for now.'

I am starting to feel panicky. This is meant to be basic? I'm not going to be able to do it. It's too hard – I can't take it all in. And what if I spell the words wrong?

'Let's try a letter,' he suggests. 'See if you can select the letter *C*.'

I try to remember how to do it. I am relieved when he reminds me.

I wait as the cursor moves between the screens. I sniff. It isn't that different to picking yes or no.

'Choose the row with a small sniff.'

C is in the first row. The cursor goes past before I can sniff so I wait for it to go through the rows and back to the first. This time I do it!

'Now another small sniff when you reach *C*,' says Mr Katz.

I've done it! *C* has appeared in the white box.

After a few minutes, with Mr Katz's patient instructions, the word *CAT* is visible at the bottom of the screen. It is slow – but I am writing words, real words, for the first time in my life.

'Do you want to type something yourself?' he asks me. 'Maybe tell us how you feel about the sniff controller.'

I panic now. What do I say? What are the best words to express how incredible this is? Amazing? Brilliant? These feel right, but they will take ages. Good? Great? Slowly I begin to sniff out the word *GREAT*. I type *G R*, but sniff too late for the next *E* and get *F*. I've typed *GRF*. What do I do now? How do I correct a mistake?

Mr Katz sees I have stopped sniffing. 'If you make an error, select this eraser symbol to get rid of the last letter,' he tells me. 'And this,' he points, 'is the space bar, if you need it.'

Yes, now I can do it! I erase the *F* and sniff the *E* instead. Then *A*, then *T*.

'If you select the red speaker button – bottom right, here – then it will speak your words,' says Mr Katz.

It takes a few sniffs to get there, but then it happens. The voice says, 'GREAT.'

'You are doing so well,' says Mr Katz. 'I think *you* are great, Jemma!'

'So do I!' says Mum. Then I hear sniffing – and it's not me. There is a sob. Mum is crying.

I begin to type, *DONT CRY*. It takes about five minutes for me to get the right letters. Mum watches. I select the speaker. Mum cries harder.

'Sorry, Jemma,' she says between sobs.

'Let me fetch you a glass of water,' says Mr Katz, handing Mum a tissue.

He leaves the room and only now do I wonder what happens next. When can I have one? It might take a while to order it, I guess. Will it have to come from Israel? I need to type something now while I have the chance.

I am about to sniff towards the *D* when Mr Katz comes back in with a glass of water and gives it to Mum.

'You have worked very hard and must be tired,' he tells me. 'It is best not to do too much the first time.' He presses something on the computer and the screen disappears. He pulls the tiny sensor tubes from my nostrils.

'No!' I want to scream. I find myself sniffing as

if to select *NO* through my nose, but of course I am disconnected now.

'I know you have waited a long time for this moment, Jemma,' says Mr Katz.

'All her life,' says Mum.

'And I am sure you are impatient to have the system at home.'

Yes, I am! He's switched it off now, but maybe he'll let me take it home with me.

'I'll have to ask you – how much does it cost?' Mum says.

I freeze. What if it is too expensive? What if I can't have it at all?

Mr Katz smiles. 'You will be surprised,' he tells Mum. 'This is unusually cheap to make. As you can see it's low tech, it's really just a plastic tube. It doesn't rely on advanced technology of the kind used for eye-gaze sensors or vocal cord hummers, although it can be connected to many devices running all kinds of software.'

So it's not too expensive! When can I have it?

'However, it is still, as I say, in the research phase and has not gone into production yet,' Mr Katz continues. 'This equipment is only a prototype.'

My heart sinks. How long will I have to wait? Can't I just have this one?

'So how soon would Jemma be able to have one at home?' Mum's asking exactly what I want to ask. I can see the disappointment in her face too.

Mr Katz's feet shuffle as he wrinkles his brow. 'I have seen, Jemma, that you can use the equipment successfully. I will speak to my team and find out if I can leave this one with you. If so, I would require you to report on your use of it as a participant in our research project. We're leaving the UK in two weeks' time, but someone in the team can bring it over to you and set it up before we go.'

The significance of this slowly sinks in. I had an opportunity to say something here and now and I've missed it. I've got so much that's so important to say. Instead of typing *CAT* I should have just typed *DAN KILLED RYAN*.

43

Mum and I have lunch in the hospital cafeteria. She leaves me by a table where I can see her and goes to get the food. I watch her pull out her purse to pay and she has a puzzled expression. She searches her bag.

'I must be going mad,' she tells me, plonking down a tray. 'I'm sure I had twenty pounds in my purse. Lucky they take card.'

I think about Olivia. Has she been taking money again?

Mum sits down next to me. 'That sniff controller's brilliant, isn't it?' she says as she spoons soup into my mouth. I am conscious of people watching, but I don't care. I wish I could tell them – all of them. I can communicate now. I can talk!

Mum phones Dad and tells him all about it. She sounds so excited. Then she listens while Dad speaks. I wish I could hear what he's saying.

*

He greets me warmly when we get home. 'Such wonderful news, Jemma. You'll be bossing us about and telling us what's what soon!'

I wish!

'All OK here?' Mum asks, as she pushes me into the kitchen. Dad follows.

'Yes. Dan phoned,' Dad tells her.

'Oh?' says Mum.

Dan – what did he want?

'Yes, he just wanted to know if we'd had any news about Sarah,' says Dad. 'He's very worried – as we all are.'

'It must be hard for him all alone,' says Mum. 'At least we have each other for support.'

I cringe inside as she says this. The only thing he's very worried about is getting caught.

'Yes, I think he sees himself as a family guy. He said he was keen to settle down with Sarah, start a family with her,' says Dad. 'He asked how the kids are doing and I told him the good news about Jemma. He sends his congratulations. He was very interested in how it works. He said to tell you, Jemma, that he'd love to come and have a chat with you some time.'

'It's nice to have something positive happening,' says Mum, sighing.

Panic surges through me as I take in what Dad said. He has told Dan that I can communicate! Dan is never going to let me tell his secret. No wonder he's *very interested*. His message to me was a threat, I know it. I feel like I was at the top of a hill, happily looking at the wonderful view, but someone has left the brake off my wheelchair and now I'm rolling down, down, faster and faster, heading straight towards a busy road.

It doesn't sound like Dad told him I might have to wait two weeks. Dan won't take the risk – he won't wait. He'll have to kill me now, won't he?

I'm scared. I will someone to stay with me at all times, but later I find myself alone in the lounge watching TV. Finn and Olivia are upstairs. Mum is clearing up from dinner. I'm not sure where Dad is.

I don't feel safe on my own. I can't stop thinking about Dan. I am alert to every little sound – though it is not as if I can do anything. I thought this sniff controller was going to change my life. I thought I had a future ahead of me, that I was going to have the chance to get to know my sister. I was stupid. The sniff controller is amazing, but Dan can't let me use it, can he?

If only I'd told Mum about Dan while I was trying it. Then someone could have done something and I wouldn't be so frightened now. I missed my chance. I know he's going to come. I can feel it.

I try to watch the quiz show on TV. I force myself to concentrate, but I don't know any of the answers. Ten, maybe fifteen minutes pass. Maybe he won't come yet. Maybe he'll wait until I'm in bed.

Then I hear a car pull up somewhere outside, a car door slam. Is that him? Could it be? I wait, look at the TV. He'll have Sarah's key – he could slip in, so quietly. A minute or two passes. There is a sound behind me. The living-room door clicks shut. That door should be open. I hear another sound. Someone took a breath. I can't see towards the door, only the TV, but I know. Someone is here, in this room, standing behind my wheelchair.

My heart beats faster. I find myself sniffing – picturing the letter board and spelling *HELP* as if a miraculous imaginary sniff controller might respond by blurting out, 'HELP! HELP!'

Nothing's happening, but I can definitely hear

breathing – very close behind me. What is he waiting for? *Come round in front of me – let me see you.*

He's moving – as if he's heard me. *I want Mum! I want Mum!* I am as helpless as a baby.

A knife glints in my face.

44

The knife – a small, sharp blade – is so close to my face it is blocking my view of anything else. I've not seen a knife like this except on telly. I think you'd call it a flick knife.

As my eyes focus, I see that the shape of the person behind it is small. The knife is held in a small purple-gloved hand. These can't be Dan's hands or gloves. The knife moves back a little. It isn't Dan.

'I know you saw,' Olivia says quietly. 'I know you saw and I know you'll tell on me.'

Olivia. Where did she get the knife? Why is she waving it at me?

'I know you saw,' she says again.

I have no idea what she's talking about.

The knife is in front of my eyes. It wavers in her shaking hands. I wish she'd drop it. It's so close. It's almost scratching my cheek. I can't control my head movements. If my head jolts the wrong way that knife will slice me.

My head jerks suddenly, as if it's heard my thoughts. I tipped away from the knife and not towards it, but I know that was pure luck.

'I've got to make sure you can't go telling tales.' There is venom in her voice though she speaks barely above a whisper. The knife is steadier. 'If you tell anyone I stole Lorraine's money they'll chuck me out of here.'

She's breathing hard. I'm in shock. It's about the money she took from Mum's purse. She didn't think I'd ever be able to tell anyone. But now she knows I will.

'I like you, Jemma,' Olivia continues, 'even though you don't do anything.' She screws up her face. 'But I can't let you tell. I'll do it quick, OK? No one will think it was me.'

She pulls the knife slowly back, ready. Surely she can't? But I can see the determination in her pressed-together lips. She means it. She's going to do it. *Mum! Mum! I need you!*

'OLIVIA!'

Suddenly Dad is there. 'What the –? For God's sake, Olivia. Where did you get that knife?'

Olivia jumps and the knife jolts wildly in front of my face. I think I feel it scrape my cheek.

'Give it to me,' says Dad.

Olivia is shaking, harder and harder, but she doesn't let go of the knife.

'Olivia. Give it to me now,' Dad says again. His voice is low, calm and serious.

Olivia drops the knife. Dad quickly grabs it and shuts it. Olivia is sobbing now, wailing. She curls up on the floor and rocks like Finn.

Saliva gathers in my mouth. I can't swallow. Would she have done it? Could she really have stabbed me? I don't know – it's hard to believe she would.

Dad's face is white with shock. He stands, paralysed for a moment, staring down at Olivia on the floor.

'Lorraine!' he yells loudly. 'Can you come in here?'

Mum runs in. 'What's happened?' Her voice is high, panicky.

'I found Olivia holding . . . holding this knife out – as if she was about to stab Jemma.'

Dad flicks the knife open and shut again for Mum to see.

'WHAT?' Mum exclaims. She comes round in front of me, looks at me anxiously and then at Olivia.

'Olivia! Calm down. What on earth were you thinking?'

Olivia is still sobbing loudly and doesn't look like she's about to calm down.

'We need that sniff controller,' says Mum. 'We need Jemma to be able to tell us what's going on.'

And she has no idea how much I need to say!

Mum sits on the floor and puts a hand on Olivia's shoulder. Olivia pushes her away. Dad is holding the knife, staring at it with a bewildered expression.

'That's not ours, is it?' Mum asks him.

'No,' Dad says firmly.

'Just tell us one thing, Olivia,' says Mum. 'Where did you get this knife?'

Olivia sobs for what feels like minutes before she finally says, 'I . . . f-found . . . it. I f-found it in the g-g-garden.'

'In *our* garden?' Dad says. 'Where exactly?'

'My ball . . . my ball went into the bushes right at the back – and . . . and . . . something was sticking up in the mud behind the shed and I p-pulled it.'

'When was this? Why didn't you tell us?' Dad asks.

'Weeks ago. I . . . I wanted to keep it,' says Olivia. 'Just in case.'

'In case of what?' Dad demands.

Olivia shrugs, but says nothing.

'Why *Jemma*?' Mum steadies her voice. 'Why were you pointing it at *her*?'

Olivia's shoulders are shaking. She begins to sob again.

'Come upstairs with me,' Mum says firmly. I wonder if Olivia will tell her the truth.

As Mum goes out I hear Sheralyn coming down. 'Is everything OK?' she asks. 'I heard shouting . . .'

Dad goes out into the hall and I can hear him telling her what's happened.

'That is one messed-up kid!' says Sheralyn.

'I know,' says Dad. 'I don't think we realised how bad it was. I'm not sure what'll happen now.'

I wonder what he means, what will happen to Olivia.

It's only when I am lying in bed later, unable to sleep, that I think about the knife. How did a knife end up buried in our garden?

Am I crazy, or could it possibly have been the knife Dan used to kill Ryan? Dan goes into the garden to smoke sometimes. Olivia might just have found the most important piece of evidence and she has no idea.

*

Olivia is staying in her room and Mum has taken some breakfast up to her. She says Olivia won't get out of bed and won't talk.

Finn is eating his square malties slowly and deliberately. He seems to be checking carefully that each one has four sides before it reaches his mouth.

Dad doesn't go to work.

'I'm going to call Mr Katz and find out when the sniff controller is coming,' he tells me as he feeds me breakfast.

It's hard to swallow. I feel stuffed so full of things I need to say there is no room for food.

I'd like to hear the call, but once I've finished eating and been wiped up, Dad goes into the living room with the phone.

He comes back looking pleased. 'Thank goodness – they say it's coming tomorrow,' he tells me. 'Someone called Mr Fogel is bringing it.'

Tomorrow.

When Mum comes down, Dad tells her about Mr Fogel. And he says that Olivia's social worker will be over in half an hour.

Mum decides I should go to school, that it is best

to keep things normal. I think they want me out of the way while they deal with Olivia.

When I get home, Olivia has gone. Mum explains that her social worker has found her somewhere else to stay for a while.

'I don't know if we'll be able to have her back here. She won't say what happened,' Mum says, shaking her head and sighing, despairingly. 'I still can't believe it. I'm so sorry, Jemma – it must have been terrifying.'

Finn is home. He isn't playing or lining things up either. He just sits rocking. I hope he is OK. I hope Olivia will be OK too.

45

The next morning, the hour and a half between Finn leaving for school and the time the sniff controller is due to arrive passes so slowly I wonder if the clock on the living-room wall has stopped. I'm starting to get a headache.

At last there is a ring at the door. He's here!

Mr Fogel introduces himself and tells me it's great to meet me. He says it with such enthusiasm it's like I'm a celebrity or something. He's short and tanned and speaks English with an American accent. He says I'll be set up in no time.

'No time' turns out to be another hour. First he has to download the communication software on to Mum's tablet. From the frown on his face I think he's having problems. What if he can't get it working? I hope I'll be able to sniff OK – be able to work it. What if the other day was a fluke and this time I can't do it at all? I try to practise while I wait. My headache gets worse.

'When you've a moment, I've got some forms I need you to sign to say you're happy for Jemma to be part of our research project,' says Mr Fogel. 'And then we'll go through the records we need you to keep.' He switches his gaze to me. 'I wanted to try this out with someone with a disability like yours and it's great to have the opportunity.'

I wish he'd get on with it. He has no idea about the urgency.

'Here we go, sorry it's taken so long,' he says finally.

He puts the sensors into my nostrils and turns the screen so that I can see it.

'Now, I know you've had a go at this – but not much chance to practise yet! We'll start with the *YES* and *NO* screen. Big sniff when the cursor is on your choice of word. Are you ready?'

I am flummoxed for a moment. I wish my head would stop thumping. How do I tell him I'm ready? Then I realise. A big sniff!

'YES,' speaks the voice.

'Great! Well done. Can you see the screen clearly enough?'

'YES,' I sniff.

Then we switch to the letter board. He gets me to spell a few words, which I do, slowly and carefully. I guess it may seem slow for someone listening, but I can do it! The thrill of it surges through me all over again. It's like a kind of magic.

'Would you mind if I asked Jemma some things in private?' Mum asks.

'Of course,' says Mr Fogel. He smiles at me as he heads off towards the kitchen.

'Jemma,' Mum says softly. 'Do you know why Olivia was threatening you?'

The seriousness of what I have to say brings me back down to earth.

'YES,' I sniff.

'Please – tell me,' says Mum.

I hesitate. I want to answer Mum, but I am not sure she is asking the most important question. I need to talk about Dan – and Sarah. Is it wrong to answer the question I want to answer rather than what Mum is asking? Will it confuse her? I feel panicky. I'm not used to having to make decisions like this!

I begin to spell. I select *D*. But when I try *A* I miss and get *B* so I've typed *DB*. How do I erase a letter? I panic. Then I remember there is an eraser key.

I select it. Now I'm back to *D*. I wish I could do this faster. At last I have sniffed *DAN*.

'Dan?' Mum repeats, clearly confused.

I ignore her. I have to think how to do a space – yes – I've selected a space. I need to explain, but I want the fewest words. I spell *RYAN* hoping she will get what I mean. Sometimes I pass the letter I need and have to wait for the cursor to go round again. I know Mum is watching. I don't know what she's thinking. I have to concentrate. I select the microphone and the voice speaks, 'DAN RYAN' – although I know Mum has already read what I've typed. Hearing it aloud I feel suddenly overwhelmed. My head spins.

'Dan Ryan?' Mum repeats. Her eyes are wide. 'Is this to do with Olivia?'

'NO,' I sniff.

'You're telling me something else. Am I right?' Mum asks.

'YES,' I select, with relief.

Mum pulls her chair close to me. 'Jemma, what are you trying to tell me about Dan and Ryan?'

'KILL,' I slowly sniff.

'What? Dan killed Ryan?' Mum asks. 'Is that what you're saying?'

'YES,' I sniff.

'How do you know this?'

'TOLD ME,' I sniff.

'Who told you?'

'DAN,' I sniff again. Then I carry on sniffing as I don't want another question. Mum waits patiently.

'KILL SARAH TOO.'

Mum's eyes are even wider. 'Jemma, wait. I need to call the police. I don't want to make you tired – I know it's a lot of effort. We'll speak to the police together.'

Mum phones the local police station and explains. When she says, 'Jemma has important information,' I feel pleased. I just hope I can explain clearly and that they'll believe me.

'They'll be here in half an hour,' Mum tells me. 'Do you want to rest?'

I am aware that I haven't answered Mum's question about Olivia. Although I'm tired and my head is spinning, that feels important too.

'OLIVIA,' I sniff.

'You want to tell me about Olivia?' Mum gives me an encouraging smile. 'I'm all ears, Jemma.'

'MONEY,' I sniff.

'Money?' Mum frowns.

'PURSE,' I sniff.

Mum hasn't got it yet. She's frowning as she tries to piece it together. I'm not being clear enough – this is so hard!

'Olivia took money from my purse?' Mum says, at last.

'YES,' I sniff.

'I thought money was going missing. I had no idea it was her . . . but why was she threatening you with a knife?'

'I SAW,' I sniff.

'She thought you would tell me?' Mum asks. 'She was scared?'

'SENT AWAY,' I sniff.

'She was scared she'd be sent away? What a mess!' says Mum. 'But we can't keep her here after what happened.'

'SAD,' I sniff.

'Yes, Jemma, I'm sad too. Do you know *why* she took the money?'

'NO,' I sniff.

Mum suddenly holds her head in her hands. She has tears in her eyes.

I feel bad. I didn't want to make Mum cry.

'Social services weren't sure about placing her here, but I convinced them – I thought we could help her.' It is Mum sniffing now. 'Maybe this wasn't the right place. And everything with Sarah – it means we've been giving her a lot less attention than she needs. What useless foster parents we are – we're supposed to be keeping you all safe!'

No! I don't want Mum to feel useless and sad!

'YOU GOOD,' I spell. 'LOVE YOU.'

'Thank you, Jemma. I love you too – so much. I'm going to phone Ben. I think he needs to be here. I still can't take all this in.'

I'm thinking about Olivia, about how terrified she was of being sent away – so terrified that she pointed a knife at me. And now her worst fears might come true. I'm sure she didn't mean to hurt me. I'm sure she wouldn't do it again. When she first came, Olivia never really felt like part of our family, but now she does. Since she's confided in me about things, I've started to feel like a big sister to her and now that I'd be able to talk to her, I could be that even more.

'OLIVIA STAY,' I tell Mum.

'What? I'm not sure, Jemma. Not after what she did . . .'

'STAY,' I repeat. 'FAMILY.'

Mum sighs and wipes her brow. She looks like she has a headache and I think her hands are shaking.

My own headache is getting worse. I wish someone would give me some painkillers. We wait. Then I suddenly realise – I can actually ask for some!

'HEAD PAIN,' I sniff.

'Of course. I'll get you some painkillers,' says Mum.

I am stunned at how easy this is. I can communicate! I really can! And I don't have to stay in pain with no one knowing. This is huge!

46

While we wait for the police and for Dad, I have a break from sniffing. It takes a lot of effort. The painkillers start working. My headache is still there, but easing off.

Mr Fogel seems unsure what to do once Mum has explained what's going on. He tells Mum he feels he should stay a while longer in case anything goes wrong with the sniff controller, but he doesn't want to be in the way. Mum reassures him and makes him a cup of coffee. He comes to sit with me in the lounge and tells me more about his research, how he is a neurobiologist specialising in olfaction – which he says is all things to do with the nose and sense of smell. They came across the idea of sniffing as a means to control things purely by chance. I am fascinated.

'I never imagined one day I'd be sitting with someone who is using the sniff controller to give a crucial witness statement to the police!' he says, giving me a big smile.

Then Mum puts on the TV and Mr Fogel and I watch a programme about people who want to move to Australia.

Mum phones Olivia's social worker to tell her what I said. She's in the kitchen, but I can hear snippets. It sounds like Olivia can't come back. I feel sad.

Dad's home. Mum starts crying when she tells him about Olivia. He hugs her and then he comes and hugs me too, so tight I worry he might pull out the sensors in my nose.

'I think I'm still in shock,' Dad says.

The police arrive. They're the same two that came when Sarah first went missing. Dad takes his newspaper into the kitchen for Mr Fogel to read while he waits. So I have Mum, Dad, PC Hunt and PC Sahin in the lounge with me. Mum explains to the police how the sniff controller works and that I have only just got it so haven't had much practice.

'Can you tell us what you told your mum?' PC Sahin asks.

It is very slow, but now I see how I can use the predictive text, which makes it slightly quicker. Even so, by the time I've spelled a word, PC Hunt is already fidgeting impatiently.

'DAN KILL RYAN,' I sniff.

PC Sahin has been watching the screen, but she looks startled as the voice finally speaks my words.

'And you know this because?' she asks.

'TOLD ME,' I spell again.

'Who told you?' she asks.

'DAN,' I sniff. 'WONT CATCH ME.'

'Dan won't catch you?' PC Sahin asks.

I thought I was doing well – I'm definitely getting faster – but I'm frustrated now. 'NO,' I sniff. I try to think how to be clearer.

'Ahh – are you telling us what Dan said?' asks PC Sahin.

I am so relieved that she has understood. 'YES,' I sniff. 'THEY WON'T CATCH ME.'

I can't believe I have managed to say a whole sentence. Suddenly I remember the knife. I didn't tell Mum that.

I sniff quickly before PC Sahin can ask another question.

'KNIFE.' Is that clear? She looks unsure, but Dad's eyes light up.

'I think I know what Jemma means – can I . . .?' Dad begins.

'I'd rather we ask the questions if you don't mind. We have to make sure we don't ask anything leading,' says PC Hunt.

'Oh, OK,' says Dad.

'You know something about a knife?' PC Sahin asks me. 'Can you tell me more about it?'

'OLIVIA KNIFE,' I sniff.

PC Hunt looks confused. I'm not explaining clearly enough. I wish I could talk more in whole sentences, but sniffing each letter is so much effort.

Dad can see I'm struggling and he ignores PC Hunt's request to keep quiet. 'Olivia found a knife in our garden,' he says. 'I'll get it.'

I hear his footsteps leave and come back a few moments later. 'Here.'

I can't see because of the angle, but I assume Dad is giving PC Hunt the knife. I hear the rustle of plastic. 'Just put it straight in here,' says PC Hunt.

'KNIFE RYAN,' I sniff.

'Does it look like the kind of knife that stabbed Ryan?' Dad asks.

'I couldn't comment on that,' says PC Hunt.

'DANS KNIFE,' I sniff.

'Do you know that?' PC Hunt asks.

'THINK,' I admit.

'Jemma, when did Dan tell you he killed Ryan?'

There's a tone in his voice as if he's not sure he believes me.

When did he tell me? I can't remember! It was weeks ago. Is it OK to say that?

'WEEKS AGO,' I sniff. I feel I need to explain more although it is taking a lot of effort.

'Do you know anything about Sarah's disappearance?' PC Sahin asks.

What can I say?

'DAN,' I sniff.

'You know Dan is responsible – or you think he might be?'

'THINK,' I sniff.

'Do you know of any reason why Dan might be responsible?'

'RICHARD,' I sniff.

PC Sahin nods, thoughtfully.

All the energy has drained from me. I need a break. I hope there are not too many more questions.

'TIRED,' I sniff.

'OK,' says PC Sahin. 'I think that's enough questions for now.'

'What happens next?' Dad asks. 'I mean, Jemma can't sign a statement or anything.'

'We'll need you to bring Jemma to the station so we can film her answering these questions,' PC Sahin explains. 'The video evidence can be used in court if needed. You have been very helpful, Jemma – very helpful indeed.'

'Well done, love,' says Mum, stroking my arm.

'TIRED,' I sniff again.

'You look washed out,' Mum says, stroking my cheek. She turns to PC Sahin. 'I really don't think she can answer all these questions again now.'

'How about you have a rest and come to the station after lunch?' PC Sahin suggests.

'Thank you, we'll do that,' says Mum.

'GET DAN,' I sniff.

'We'll certainly be making further enquiries,' she assures me.

I've done it! I've told them – although I wish I didn't

have to do it all over again for the video. At least they are taking me seriously. The police will arrest Dan and they'll find out what happened to Sarah. I feel ecstatic at being able to communicate something so important.

'Do you want to have a lie-down?' Mum asks, when they've gone.

'YES,' I sniff.

'It's so nice to be able to ask you what you want rather than decide for you,' she says as she wheels me into my bedroom.

But lying there on my bed, I couldn't sleep. My head felt like it was full of bees buzzing round and round. I couldn't switch off until I knew the police had locked Dan up.

I heard Mr Fogel leave and wished I'd said goodbye to him properly and told him how grateful I was – though I could hear Mum and Dad thanking him again and again.

By the time I'd been to the police station with Mum and gone through all the questions again, I felt like I'd got nothing left. I wish I'd managed to ask if they'd arrested Dan yet, but answering the questions used up all my energy.

As we left the police station, we passed a police car arriving. Maybe Dan was in it – I wish I could have seen.

Back home I was able to ask to lie down again. Mum took out the sniff controller tube and that time I fell asleep instantly.

Now I'm awake, and I have no idea how much time has passed. I can hear Mum's voice. I think she's in the kitchen on the phone. I try to listen, but I can't hear what Mum's saying or work out who she's talking to. Is it the police?

Mum doesn't come. I'm lying here, waiting and waiting.

Finally her head appears round the door.

'I was feeling impatient wondering what was happening,' she tells me, 'so I called the station.' She smiles. 'They've got him, Jemma! The police have got Dan. They're questioning him now.'

I'm so relieved. *They've got him!* I wish I could have seen his face when he opened the door to them.

But what about Sarah?

47

Mum sits me up gently and moves me into my wheelchair. She pushes me into the lounge before connecting the sniff controller. It takes a few tries to get the tube up my nose properly. 'We'll get some kind of clamp so we can attach the tablet to your chair,' she tells me as she props it up on a tray so I can see it. I am impatient, eager to ask about Sarah.

'SARAH?' I finally sniff.

'No news yet,' says Mum, 'but give them a chance, Jemma. Would you like a drink? I'm going to make myself a cup of tea.'

'WATER,' I sniff. It still feels incredible to be able to ask for things.

I think about Dan, imagining him being questioned. I hope he's squirming in his chair, stuck for words. I'd love him to know what it's like when you can't speak. I hope he's scared too – really scared.

Mum brings the drinks, sits down near me

and helps me drink the water from a straw.

'It must have been terrible for you,' she says as she sips her tea, 'knowing all that and not being able to tell us.'

'YES,' I sniff slowly.

'And we were all taken in by him, apart from you.'

'YES,' I sniff. Though I know if I had been able to talk, Dan would never have shared his secret with me.

'SARAH?' I ask again, after dinner.

'I'll phone the station and see if there's any update,' Mum tells me.

'WANT,' I sniff.

'What do you want, Jemma?' she asks.

'HEAR,' I continue.

'Of course,' says Mum. She fiddles with the phone, turning on the loudspeaker.

I wait while Mum gets through to PC Hunt.

'We wondered if there was any news about Sarah,' Mum asks.

'Well,' says PC Hunt, 'we've talked to Dan Harris, but unfortunately we've found no reason to hold him.'

'Oh?' says Mum.

'He has an alibi for the evening Ryan was killed and we have no other evidence against him. There is nothing to indicate he is connected with Sarah's disappearance either. He has an alibi for that night too. So we've had to let him go.'

'Goodness,' says Mum.

My breath comes fast. I don't believe it. The police have made a mistake. Dan must've lied about his alibis. I know he did it. I know!

'But Jemma was so sure,' Mum says quietly. 'I don't believe she was making it up.'

'It wasn't exactly your average witness statement,' PC Hunt says. 'She's never spoken before. Maybe she got overexcited – started making up stories. Maybe it's all jumbled in her head.'

He doesn't believe a word I said! He'd rather believe Dan. *Making up stories . . . jumbled in her head.* How dare he say that?

Mum glances at me and I think she's wishing she hadn't put the loudspeaker on. I hope she doesn't turn it off now.

'TRUE,' I sniff to Mum. 'WAS DAN.'

'I think Jemma believed what she told you to be true,' Mum tells PC Hunt. 'Dan may have been having a laugh with her, but I'm sure Jemma heard what she says she heard.'

'You know her best, of course, but like I said – it's a weird situation. Perhaps she just wanted something dramatic to say. She's a teenager, after all.'

Even Mum is speechless at this. I can speak, but I don't know what to say either.

'What about the knife?' Mum suddenly asks. 'Was it the one that killed Ryan?'

'The knife will be tested,' PC Hunt tells her.

'And Sarah?' asks Mum.

'Sarah remains on the missing persons list. Hopefully in time she will make contact. We'll keep you informed.'

Mum comes off the phone and looks at me. 'Are you all right, Jemma?'

I am seething. I want this tube out of my nose – but I don't feel like sniffing, not even to say that. How can he have an alibi? It must be a lie. Why can't the police see through him? They'd rather believe him than me – just because I'm in a wheelchair and he's standing on his own two feet. I know I'm right. The way PC Hunt spoke about me was utterly humiliating.

'Jemma?' Mum asks again.

I don't answer. I'm not sniffing again, not ever. I have nothing more to say.

48

'Jemma's had a shock,' I hear Mum saying. It's the next morning and she's on the phone to Mr Fogel. 'I'm not sure if she's stopped trying to sniff or whether the sniff controller's stopped working,' she tells him. There's a pause. 'OK,' Mum says. 'I'll contact you in a few days. We'll see what happens. Thank you.'

Surely Mum realises. She doesn't really think it's broken, does she?

At breakfast Dad tries to encourage me to speak. I don't. I *won't*. Breakfast is very quiet. No Sarah and no Olivia either. I miss her – in a weird way I even miss her tantrums.

After breakfast, Finn has his box of matchsticks and is lining them up against the kitchen wall when he accidentally steps on the box and the matches spill. He is horrified, frantically trying to pick them up and put them back, but he's trying to do it too fast and some of them spill out again.

This is how I feel – like everything's spilling out, all over the place. Like Finn, I want life to all be straight lines for a change.

'Here, let me help you, Finn,' Dad says gently. Finn doesn't react, but he doesn't stop Dad either. Soon the matches are all back in the box and Finn goes back to lining them up.

'Jemma,' Dad says, sitting beside me and touching my arm. 'You told the police what you knew. It isn't your fault that Dan lied to you. What he did was very unkind.'

Unkind. I still can't believe it was a lie – not when I think about what he said when he learned there might be a way for me to communicate.

'Don't let that spoil things. You can talk to us, Jemma! It's incredible. Don't let Dan or the police take that away.'

They're not taking it away. I just don't want to do it any more. That's all.

By the evening there is no further news and I am still not sniffing. Dad phones Kate, but she has nothing to report.

'Talk to me, Jemma,' Mum begs, as she clears up

from dinner. 'Tell me how you're feeling. I know it must be tough.'

She has no idea how tough. And no, I'm not talking, not to anyone.

'What would cheer you up?' Mum asks.

Dan in prison, finding Sarah, everything getting back to normal – but that's not going to happen, is it? Nothing will cheer me up.

By bedtime I have still not sniffed at all.

'What about Jodi?' Mum suggests gently, putting an arm round my shoulder. 'Would you like to see her?'

My sister. I don't feel like talking, but maybe . . . Jodi. That's different. Now that Mum's said it, I know she's right. Mum has said the only thing that might possibly make me feel a little better.

But she's given up waiting for me to answer. She's stood up and is walking out of the room.

'YES,' I sniff.

49

I am waiting for Jodi. Yesterday passed so slowly and now she's late and I'm scared she's changed her mind. Apart from sniffing 'YES' to seeing Jodi, I have kept quiet. Dad's attached the tablet to my wheelchair with a clamp so I can speak whenever I want to, but I still don't feel like talking. I'm not even sure I'm going to talk to Jodi. I want to see her, though.

We wait. Where is she? She was meant to be here half an hour ago.

Mum looks at her watch. 'I'll text her in a minute if she's still not arrived,' she tells me.

Then I hear the bell, and Mum goes to answer the door.

'Hi, Jodi,' I hear her say.

'So sorry I'm late!' Jodi replies.

'Don't worry. Jemma will be delighted that you're here,' says Mum. 'Come through.'

'I'm a bit nervous,' I hear Jodi say. 'This sniff thing

– how does it work? Will I need to do anything?'

I don't want Jodi to be nervous.

'It's easy,' says Mum. 'Jemma does it all! We'll show you. She might not say much, though.'

Finally they come in from the hallway. Mum points Jodi towards the sofa.

She turns me so I'll be facing Jodi, who sits down a little awkwardly.

'Hi, Jemma. So sorry I'm late! The bus took *forever* – the traffic was terrible.'

'I'll get you a drink,' Mum tells her. 'What would you like? Tea? Coke?'

'Coke, please,' says Jodi.

Mum goes out. Jodi leans towards me. 'Now, show me how this thing works,' she says. 'I'm so excited that you can speak!'

Her excitement is infectious. My lovely sister is here and I can talk to her. I want to – I really do.

'HAPPY,' I sniff slowly.

'Wow! That's so cool,' she says, watching patiently as the letters appear and the voice finally speaks. 'I'm so happy to see you too, Jemma!'

There's an awkward pause. I guess it's my turn to speak. What do I say? My mind goes blank.

Maybe Jodi will say something else – but she doesn't. I have to say something. Now I understand what Professor Spalding meant about learning to speak. Even though I can think clearly and my thoughts just come into my head with no effort, with speech I have to decide what to say and choose the words. And then with AAC I need to find the shortest words, to use the least effort to express what I want to say. I feel panicky. I say the only thing that comes into my head.

'SAD SARAH,' I tell Jodi. It takes me a long time to get all this out.

'Sarah's sad? No, you're sad about Sarah? You must miss her so much.'

'YES,' I sniff. Jodi gets it – she understands me!

There's another pause. Jodi's not saying anything. I realise I should ask her something, but I can't think what.

'Actually, I've had quite a week myself,' she tells me. 'I split up with Jack. We'd only been going out for a month, but I really liked him. He went off with another girl from my class.'

'IDIOT,' I sniff and Jodi bursts out laughing. It's brilliant that I can make her laugh.

'NEW BOY,' I sniff.

Jodi smiles. 'I need a new boyfriend? Yes, actually there is a boy I've got my eye on . . . He's in the year above.'

'GOOD LUCK,' I sniff.

'Ha ha – thanks!' Jodi grins. 'I'll let you know how it goes! Is there anyone you fancy, Jemma?'

I am about to sniff 'no' but then I remember. Actually, there is.

'LEO GLOWLIGHT,' I tell her.

'You like Glowlight too! You're right. He's awesome!' Jodi laughs.

A strange snort comes from my throat. I think I am actually laughing too!

'LOVE YOU JODI,' I sniff.

'I love you too, Jemma,' Jodi tells me. 'It's so cool that we can talk properly now!'

Mum comes back with a Coke for Jodi and an apple juice for me. She's taken a while – maybe she was just giving us some time to talk. She puts the straw in my cup and holds it up.

'I can do that,' says Jodi.

'I'll leave you to it, then,' says Mum, smiling. 'Just call me if you need anything.'

Mum's gone. Jodi holds my cup and eases the straw into my mouth. I sip.

She puts the drink down. She is quiet again. I'm tired from all the sniffing, but I don't want to stop. Only I'm not sure what to say.

'FIND SARAH,' I sniff.

'It must be awful not knowing what's happened,' says Jodi. She strokes my hand. 'I wish there was something I could do to help, but I think you'll have to leave it to the police.'

'NO GOOD,' I tell her.

She laughs. 'It's their job – I'm sure they're trying their best.'

'WE FIND HER,' I sniff. 'YOU ME.'

'But . . . how?'

'TRY,' I sniff.

'OK, then.' Jodi sighs and leans forward. 'You must've known Sarah so well, better than anyone, maybe. Think about everything you know, Jemma. Tell me if you can think of anything – *anything* – at all that might help.'

I think hard. I love it that Jodi is listening. But what do I know that I haven't already told the police?

'SARAH LOVE DAN,' I sniff. I'm pleased that I'm

already getting faster at it, though it still takes me a long time.

'OK . . .' she says, frowning.

'DAN BAD MAN,' I sniff.

'But he didn't kill Ryan,' says Jodi.

'DID,' I sniff, 'AND HE GOT SARAH.'

'Come on, then.' She smiles. 'How are we going to prove it? What else do you know?'

I try to remember everything I know about Dan, every time that he came to the house. The things he said to me flash through my head, making me shudder. What do I know that could help? Surely there's something, but I just can't think.

Jodi sits waiting, fiddling with a pretty ring on her finger. Her phone starts buzzing. She looks at it and switches it off. 'Nothing important,' she says, smiling.

I have a sudden memory – Dan standing in here, his mobile ringing. Billy – it was Billy. Could he know something?'

'DAN FRIEND BILLY,' I sniff.

'Do the police know about him?' Jodi asks.

'NO,' I sniff. I don't know for certain, but I don't think so.

'What do you know about Billy?' she asks.

I remember what Sarah called him. 'BILLY NO BRAINS.'

Jodi laughs. 'Oh yeah?

'BIG HEAD BIG BRAIN?'

'Big heads don't always equal big brains, Jemma,' Jodi laughs.

'DAN PHONE BILLY,' I continue.

'You heard him? What did he say?'

I try to remember. It wasn't anything that interesting or it would have stuck in my mind. Then it comes to me. 'BEHIND THE CO OP.'

'Interesting,' says Jodi. 'What do you think he meant was behind the Co-op?'

'DON'T KNOW,' I sniff. This is hard work. I can't keep sniffing like this. It's wearing me out. But then I have another thought. 'YOU ME GO.'

'Go where?'

'CO OP,' I sniff. 'NOT FAR.'

'You really think this might be important?'

'YES.'

Jodi smiles at me. 'OK, then.'

50

She goes into the kitchen and asks Mum if she can take me for a walk. Mum sounds pleased and a minute later she comes in with my coat.

'Don't be out too long. It still gets dark so early. Oh, and if you pass the Tesco Local, would you mind picking up a few onions for me?' Mum asks her. 'Here, I'll give you the money.'

'Sure,' says Jodi. 'I've never pushed a wheelchair before,' she adds, suddenly sounding nervous. I hope she's not going to change her mind.

'Jemma's well strapped in,' Mum tells her. 'Going up and down kerbs is the only tricky thing. Come outside and I'll give you a demo.'

Soon we are off! I am out with my sister. I jerk the first couple of times we go down a kerb, but then Jodi gets the hang of it. She seems to be enjoying it. She starts to run, pushing me fast so the wind zooms past my face. This is great!

I direct her to the Co-op. It's not near the Tesco Local, but we can get Mum's onions there. Left then second right. Then all the way to the other end of the road and left. She stops at each junction and I tell her which way to go. It's not complicated, but I hope I'm doing it right. I've only been there a couple of times – and I've never given directions before.

To my relief, the Co op comes into view. This part of town is a bit run-down and dingy. There are some parades of terraced houses, but it's mostly flats, warehouses and office blocks. Some of the buildings look derelict and have boarded-up windows. Others have scaffolding round them. There are very few people around. I start to feel nervous. The tablet attached to my wheelchair might look very tempting to a thief. And I got so carried away with the idea of coming here, I didn't actually think about what we'd do when we got here.

Jodi stops outside the Co-op. 'What now, Jemma?'

I don't know what to say. Jodi turns me right and left so I can see in both directions. It doesn't help much. Jodi stops, and I stare at the door to the Co-op, thinking. Then I remember what Dan said.

'BEHIND,' I sniff.

‘OK – here we go,’ she says.

Round the back of the Co-op there are bins. Lots of bins. Some of them are overflowing.

‘Hmmm,’ says Jodi. She turns me slowly so I can see all the way round.

There is the delivery entrance for the Co-op, a few spaces for cars to park. Not much else. No houses or buildings or any sort of place that could hold a clue.

‘Shall we go?’ Jodi asks me.

I am about to sniff ‘YES’. This was a stupid idea and I wish we’d never come. What Dan said to Billy, it was the only thing I could remember and I thought it might mean something. That was ridiculous, wasn’t it? But I am reluctant to leave.

‘TURN,’ I ask.

‘OK.’

Again Jodi turns me. There’s a passageway between two tall buildings. It looks dark and uninviting, but I think we should investigate. It’s hard for me to get Jodi to stop in the right place so she’ll see where I mean.

‘Well?’ she asks.

‘TURN,’ I repeat.

She turns me twice more and I am starting to

feel giddy before we are finally pointing in the right direction.

'THAT WAY,' I sniff.

'OK,' she says. 'We'll have a look and then we'll go.'

The buildings tower above us as Jodi pushes me along the path between them, their flat roofs merging with the grey-black of the late afternoon sky. I feel very small. There is no pavement so I hope no cars choose this moment to appear. We come out into a narrow yard with a row of run-down garages. A few have closed doors, but some are hanging off and some have no doors at all. The nearest open one has stacks of bricks inside and another has a pile of wooden planks. Jodi pushes me nearer. There is a smell like unclean toilets. It's getting darker too.

'I don't like it here,' says Jodi. 'Can we go now?'

I don't like it here either, but I'm reluctant to leave. I can't exactly ask Jodi to look in those creepy garages. 'YES,' I tell her. 'SORRY.'

'It's OK,' she says. 'It was worth a look, if you thought it might be important. I'm not sure what we were looking for, though.'

She is pushing me back towards the passage when I hear a sound behind us – a clang of metal

– but Jodi doesn't seem to hear and I can't turn to look. We're moving so I can't tell her to stop. It was probably nothing.

We're nearly at the gap between the buildings when I hear voices – men's voices. They're coming from the path we are heading to – and they are getting closer. Jodi instinctively pulls me back and round the side of the garages so they won't see us. I suddenly feel very vulnerable. What if they find us?

I want to know what's happening, but Jodi doesn't dare risk putting her head out in case she is seen. I hope I can keep quiet – I can't help making sounds sometimes. The more I think about trying to keep quiet the more I worry a sound will come out. I try not to think about it – to focus on listening as the voices come nearer.

'I don't like it,' says one man. 'It's gone on too long.'

The voice sounds familiar. It could be Billy – it sounds like him, though the tone is anxious, not relaxed like when I met him. It could easily be a stranger.

'Quit whining,' says another voice.

That's Dan. Now I'm sure it's Billy too. I can barely breathe.

'You've gotta let her go, man!' says Billy, pleadingly. 'We . . . we can't just keep her . . .'

'I told you to shut it! I'll sort it, right?' says Dan.

'What . . . what do you mean?' says Billy.

'Don't know why you're scared after what you . . .'

I don't catch the end of the sentence. They're moving away from us now. I hear the clink of keys. Then the sound of one of the garage doors lifting and going down again.

I've got to get Jodi to call the police. She's got to do it quickly. But my breathing's gone all weird and I can't sniff. I get a surge of panic.

Jodi whispers to me. 'Is that them? Were they talking about Sarah?'

'YES.' The word appears on the screen, but I am careful not to select the speaker button. It's hard to sniff accurately. I have to slow down even though I want to get the words out fast. 'POLICE.'

I can see Jodi hesitating. Maybe she's wondering if it's safe to call from here or if it is even more dangerous to move in case they come out and spot us.

Jodi takes out her mobile. 'Police,' she says quietly, when the call connects. There's another pause. 'We think someone's being held prisoner. Behind the Co-op on Redding Road – the derelict garages. We're too scared to move. Two of us. My sister's in a wheelchair.' She listens, then hangs up.

'They're coming,' she whispers.

I'm starting to feel shivery. What if Dan heard? What if he finds us here?

We wait. The buildings around us seem to creak and groan. Apart from that it is quiet. Did the police believe Jodi? Did they realise the urgency?

At last! There is the crunch of tyres and the sound of an engine. The police car pauses at our end of the gap, headlights lighting the grey tarmac. Jodi runs out. I can't see what's happening. I hear the car doors opening, footsteps.

There's a muffled scream – a woman's scream.

Then I hear the voice.

'Police!'

I hear shouting, banging. I'm terrified. I can't see Jodi. I can't see anything. The police car is in the way.

It feels like an age and my heart is thudding like a drum. What's happening? *What?*

Then I hear the voice again. 'Ambulance needed, garages on Redding Road, behind the Co-op.'

A gurgling noise comes from my throat. *No!* Then I hear, 'Woman in her twenties, conscious but injured.'

She's alive! Sarah's alive!

Jodi is back. She pushes me out into the yard, which is now action-packed, like something from a film. There are more flashing lights. A police van is here now too. A man is in handcuffs, getting in the back. I can't see well, but I think it's Billy.

'Move back,' a policeman tells us. Then suddenly Dan is in front of me. He's handcuffed too. His eyes meet mine. His mouth drops open in astonishment.

I feel hot and cold all at once. *I got you, Dan. I got you!*

And then I realise – I can say something. At last, I can say something to Dan. I start to sniff.

'FREAK.'

Dan's shoulders jolt in surprise and his eyes are wide. He turns away and the policeman blocks my view as he gets into the van. An ambulance arrives, and there is hardly space for it to park. The paramedics jump out and I wait. I desperately want to see Sarah. But she doesn't appear. They're taking ages. How badly hurt is she? The police are saying we should go home. A policeman offers to come with us, but Jodi says no, it's not far to walk. They say they'll take statements from us later. They are talking to Jodi as if I am not there.

'We came because of Jemma,' Jodi says. 'Something she overheard. She thought it might be important and wanted to check it out.'

'Well, it was a really risky thing to do,' says the police officer, 'but you did well, both of you.'

When we reach home, Jodi rings the bell and Mum opens the door, smiling. 'You were a while. Everything OK?'

Jodi doesn't speak. I think the shock of everything has suddenly hit her.

'Did you manage to get the onions?' asks Mum.

51

'NO,' I sniff. 'GOT DAN.'

'You did what?' Mum asks as we make our way into the kitchen.

'We forgot the onions, but the police have got Dan,' Jodi tells Mum. 'Because of Jemma.'

Mum's mouth opens, but she can't speak.

'FOUND SARAH,' I tell Mum.

'Is she . . .?' Mum asks.

'She's alive,' says Jodi.

Mum listens to our story. A police officer arrives at the door. I recognise him from the garages. He says he is DS Bell and he wants to ask me and Jodi some questions. He wants us to come to the station so they can video my answers. I have done so much sniffing today I can barely stay awake. I ask how Sarah is, but all he can say is that she's been taken to hospital, which I already know.

At least at the police station DS Bell questions

me as if he believes everything I'm saying. He's very different to PC Hunt.

When we're finished, Mum drops Jodi at her house and takes me home. I am able to tell her I want to sit in the lounge with some gentle music on. I think if she hadn't been able to ask me she would have put me to bed, but my mind is whirring far too much to sleep.

I can't believe what just happened. What Dan did – it makes me sick. Keeping Sarah locked up in a garage all these weeks, and coming round here, pretending he was worried about her. And what if we hadn't been there at that moment? I think how we nearly turned back. We were about to. I shudder. Poor Sarah – I can't imagine what it was like locked in there. She must have been desperate. She must have wondered if she'd ever get out.

Then I think about what *I* did. I can hardly believe that either. Dan thought I was powerless, but I wasn't. I knew I wanted to communicate, but I never really thought about the power it would give me. I feel different – like I have a new inner strength. Even so, I realise there are some things you just can't control – no one can, like the way other people behave.

*

We have fish and chips for dinner and I manage to sniff, 'KETCHUP.' Mum looks at me in surprise before mashing some ketchup into my chips. Mum fills Dad in on everything that's happened. Dad shakes his head in disbelief.

I watch Finn lining up his chips in neat rows on his plate. Next minute he's pushed the plate away and is banging his head on the table.

'Finn! Stop that,' Dad tells him. 'What's the matter?'

I look – and I can see what's wrong. Finn is one chip short. As he leaned over the plate, a chip attached itself to his jumper and is still hanging below his elbow.

I have to swallow my mouthful and then I sniff, 'FINN.'

His head jerks up in surprise at the computer voice saying his name. He looks bewildered. He doesn't seem sure where it's coming from.

I select the speaker again. 'FINN. FINN.' Until he looks at me

'CHIP JUMPER,' I tell him. Finn looks at his jumper and suddenly sees the chip. He pulls it off and puts it back in line on his plate.

'Well done, Jemma,' says Dad.

This is the first thing I have said to Finn. He glances up at me, meeting my eyes for just a second. He's smiling.

The next day Mum is meant to be coming with me to school to show my teachers how the sniff controller works. I feel completely drained after yesterday, though, and tell her I don't feel up to school.

'Don't worry,' says Mum. 'Stay home today and rest. I'll come and show them another day.'

It is late afternoon when the phone rings. Mum answers it and then runs into the lounge.

'Jemma, that was Paula. The police have got the DNA results back from the knife. Someone had tried to clean it with bleach, apparently, but there were still tiny specks of blood. It *was* the knife that killed Ryan!'

'DAN,' I sniff.

'No,' says Mum. 'Dan's alibi for that night was backed up by CCTV. He was miles away at a casino, or something. But what they have discovered is that a hair found on Ryan's clothing belongs to Billy. He's the main suspect now, Paula says.'

'WHY BILLY?' I sniff. It still doesn't make sense.

If Billy killed Ryan, why did Dan make me think he did it?

'I've no idea why Billy did it,' says Mum.

'SARAH?' I ask.

'I've spoken to Kate,' says Mum. 'They're keeping her in hospital for a few days, but it sounds like she'll be OK.'

I am so relieved. I just want her back here.

52

Sarah is coming! There's been a weird atmosphere at home these last few days – such a mixture of things, like one of Mum's 'everything goes in' stews. We're all pleased and relieved that Sarah's been found, that she's alive – but shocked too, and horrified at what she's been through. I am less shocked than Mum and Dad because I knew what Dan was like – but I still feel dreadful thinking about all those days Sarah was locked in that garage. If I only I could have told them sooner, if only I could have warned Sarah, she might not have had to go through all that.

Kate wanted Sarah to go and stay with her, but Sarah wanted to come here. I am worried about what state she'll be in, how she'll be feeling – but I can't wait for her to be back. Once Sarah is here things will feel a bit more normal again.

I hear the bell. My heart starts beating so fast. Sarah. *Sarah!* But the voice isn't Sarah's. It's Paula.

'Jemma,' says Paula, as she comes into the lounge. 'Thank you so much! It's down to you that they got him, that evil man.'

'Do they know why did Billy did it?' Mum asks her.

'He's a thief,' Paula tells us. 'The police have connected him to a string of thefts from jewellers. I suspected my Ryan had got himself into some kind of mess. They think he was helping out with raids and decided to keep some of the stuff himself. And Billy wasn't having that.'

Mum is shaking her head as she takes all this in.

Paula carries on. 'And I'm thinking that if Dan knew what Billy had done, he used it to make Billy help him kidnap Sarah.'

There's a pause as all of this sinks in.

'SARAH COMING,' I sniff.

'Really?' says Paula. 'That's wonderful! The poor girl – it's dreadful to think . . .'

'Yes, she should be here soon,' Mum says, looking at her watch. 'It's because of Jemma that they found Sarah too, of course.'

Mum smiles at me.

'Anyway, I won't stick around if you're expecting Sarah,' Paula says, standing up. 'I just wanted to fill you in – and to thank you, Jemma. I'll be off.'

Paula has only been gone two minutes when the doorbell rings again.

So many times I've imagined her walking through the door. And here she is.

I knew she might look different after going through something so horrific, but this doesn't stop the shock when I see her. She looks thinner. Her hair is lank, her skin spotty and her eyes have a scary emptiness. She does manage a tiny smile when she sees me. She opens her mouth as if to speak, but she coughs. The cough is chesty and hollow and it feels like it will never stop.

'Jemma, it's so good to see you,' she finally croaks. 'Thank you . . . for everything.' Her voice is sad and small, and even though I know she's pleased to see me, it feels like part of her is somewhere else.

Now is my chance – my chance to communicate with Sarah for the first time. 'LOVE YOU SARAH,' I sniff.

She manages a slightly bigger smile. 'Wow. Look at you talking!'

There's a silence. No one really knows what to say. She knows – she must know – we care about her so much. But you can't just fix something like this.

Sarah turns to Mum. 'I'll go and have a shower, if that's OK?' she says. 'I had showers at the hospital of course, but I don't feel clean. I can't . . .'

'Have a shower, love – take as long as you want,' says Mum.

She disappears upstairs. It is Sarah – but it isn't. Things aren't going to be the same. And of course I knew that, deep down. It will be good that I can speak, though – I want to help her feel better.

Sarah doesn't come down for about an hour. I wait and wait. She looks better, but her face still has an emptiness.

'Cup of tea?' asks Mum.

'Thank you.' Sarah nods.

Mum goes into the kitchen to make it and Sarah sits down with me.

'I can't believe I was so wrong about him,' she says quietly. 'I expect you knew, Jemma. I bet you've got more sense than me.'

'I KNEW,' I tell her.

'I should have stuck with Richard – sweet Richard. I don't know what got into me.'

Mum comes in at the end of this.

'He was a charmer, Dan,' says Mum. 'Anyone can fall for a charmer.'

'He said I was his and his alone, like he owned me.' Sarah looks shaky.

'Don't talk about it now unless you want to,' says Mum, touching her shoulder gently.

Sarah takes a sip of tea and then coughs that chesty cough again.

'Have they given you something for that cough?' Mum asks.

Sarah nods. 'I've got antibiotics. It was freezing and draughty in that garage.'

'How could he do it – treat you like that?' Mum's voice is bitter. 'He deceived us all, you know.'

I wasn't taken in, but I don't bother to point this out.

'You're welcome to stay here and rest up,' says Mum. 'Take all the time you need to recover. It must've been a horrendous ordeal.'

'Thanks,' says Sarah. She rubs her eyes. 'Look – I don't . . . this, this is so hard . . . I hope you'll all understand – but . . .'

I brace myself as Sarah pauses. But *what*?

Sarah sighs. 'I need space and time to sort myself

out. I wanted to come here because this is my home – but I'm only staying a few days. Then I'll go to my sister's. I need time to think.'

'WANT YOU STAY,' I sniff. 'I LOOK AFTER YOU.'

Sarah gives a little gasp. 'That is so sweet, Jemma. I love you. This – it's not to do with you, I promise. I . . . I don't know. I just need space.'

As I try to take in this awful news, Sarah tells us that Richard visited her in hospital yesterday.

'He feels so bad about not seeing me into the house after the concert,' she says. 'I tried to say he's got nothing to feel bad about – I was cheating on him!'

'I don't think you or Richard should worry yourselves about that now, not after everything . . .' Mum sighs. 'What happened – when you got out of the car, after the concert?' she asks. Then she puts her hand over her mouth. 'I'm sorry, I shouldn't have asked. I'm sure you don't want to talk about it.'

'It's OK,' says Sarah. 'I got to the front door and just as I went to put the key in, a hand went over my mouth. Dan was holding me tight, forcing me to walk, and he bundled me into a car and drove me to that garage. He'd found out about Richard and he was angry – so angry! But I deserved it, didn't I?' Sarah breaks into sobs.

'You can't think that!' says Mum, just as I sniff, 'NO.'

'Dan may have felt angry, but that could never make it OK – what he did,' says Mum. Her fists are clenched.

Sarah bursts into tears. Mum is by her side in a second. She puts her arm round Sarah and grabs some tissues from the table. I try to think of something I can say.

But I guess sometimes there is nothing you can say. It's just being there that's important.

I can't take in that she's leaving. Is she going to come back? I have wanted her back so much. I know the most important thing is that she's OK – and that she does what she needs to do right now. I'm trying not to think about myself in this, but I don't want her to go, not now. Not straight away.

Later, I am lying in bed and overhear Mum and Dad talking in the kitchen. Sarah has gone to bed early.

'I can't bear thinking about it,' Mum says, 'her being locked up in that garage all that time. At least she says he didn't lay a finger on her.'

'No, just left her there to rot,' Dad says sourly.

'Acted like he was doing her a favour by bringing a bit of food and water. Expecting her to be grateful – can you imagine?' says Mum. 'I'm not surprised she wants a break.'

'Maybe we need a break too,' Dad says.

I feel a flash of alarm. What is he saying?

'We've had such a tough few months,' Dad continues. 'Jemma could go to that college. I'm sure she'll get on well now she has the sniff controller. Someone else could take Finn.'

'No!' says Mum.

I am relieved that she sounds so horrified.

'You know how he hates change – and Jemma too,' says Mum. 'They need us.'

'We're only good for them if we are in a good state ourselves. And I'm not sure we are,' says Dad.

Then I hear Mum crying.

I knew things weren't going to stay the same, but *Mum and Dad*? I thought they'd always be here. How wrong could I be?

53

All night my mind tosses and turns even though my body can't. I thought my world was going to be back to normal now that Dan is in custody. I thought my home, my 'nest' would be safe – with Mum and Dad and Sarah and Finn and the chance to get to know my sister Jodi too.

I can speak. I told Mum to let Olivia stay, and they've sent her away. I told Sarah I wanted her to stay and I love her – but it made no difference. So what is the point?

I am awake when Mum comes to turn me. I realise Sarah may never do it again; never turn me, never read to me, never paint my nails, never confide her secrets.

In the morning Mum puts my sniff-controller tubes up my nose, but I have nothing to say. I can't bear what's happening and I don't even answer when Mum asks me if I am OK.

Sarah doesn't come down for breakfast. Mum

takes up a tray with coffee and toast.

'Talk to me, Jemma,' Mum says gently, when she comes down. 'You can tell me how you feel and what you're thinking now. Let me try to help.'

I know I am being mean, but I don't feel like communicating. It is an effort to do it and I don't even know what to say.

'Are you upset about Sarah?' Mum asks me.

I rouse myself to sniff *Y* and then select *YES* from the predictive text.

'I know,' says Mum. 'We got her back and now she's going again. It's so hard, isn't it? But we'll cope. This is what she needs – and whatever happens, she's part of our family. And we'll make sure you always have the care you need, Jemma.'

She's looking at me as if she's waiting for a response.

I want to ask, 'Are you going to stop fostering?' but I'm too scared. What if she says yes?

I watch as Mum empties the dishwasher. I feel like I have been emptied too.

'Come on, I'm taking you somewhere,' says Mum.

'WHERE,' I sniff.

'Wait and see,' says Mum.

I am soon in the car with Mum. I want to know

where we're going. We drive for about ten minutes. I am shocked when she parks outside the police station. Surely there are no more questions. I've told the police everything I know. Mum lowers the ramp and wheels me out of the car, pushing me towards the entrance.

'WHY HERE,' I sniff. 'GO HOME.'

'You'll see,' says Mum.

Mum speaks to the woman behind the screen and a police officer comes out.

'Mrs Bryant! Jemma! I'm so glad you're here.'

I recognise his voice before he comes round in front so I can see him. It's PC Hunt, the one who said I invented my story. He's the last person I want to see. He may be glad I'm here, but I'm not.

'Come through,' he says.

'NO,' I sniff, but Mum ignores me. PC Hunt smiles at her as he holds a door open and she pushes me through.

He's got nothing to smile about as far as I'm concerned.

He leads us into a room and moves a chair aside to make room for my wheelchair. He holds a chair out for Mum and then sits down opposite us and strokes his chin.

'GO HOME,' I sniff.

'I can see why you're not keen to be here,' says PC Hunt. 'But I asked your mum to bring you for a reason. I have something important to say to you.'

I had something important to say to you *last week,* I think. *But look how that turned out.*

'I wanted to apologise to you, face to face,' he says. He's looking straight into my eyes and he looks serious. 'This crime has been solved thanks to you. I know you heard some things I said on the phone to your mum, things I should never have said. I'm sorry if I upset you.'

'YOU DID,' I sniff. I'm not letting him off that easily.

He smiles awkwardly. 'You found Sarah – and Dan and Billy are locked up now thanks to your help.'

'I SAID DAN,' I remind him. 'NO LISTEN.'

'Yes, you were right – and in more ways than you know.'

What does he mean? I am interested now.

'Although Dan didn't actually kill Ryan Blake,' he goes on, 'we now believe Dan got Billy to do it for him.'

I begin to sniff. 'DAN MADE.'

PC Hunt nods. 'Exactly. Dan made Billy do it.'

Billy has finally agreed to help us with our enquiries. He says he was working for Dan, and Ryan was too. He told us that when Dan found out Ryan was keeping some of the stolen goods he was furious – he wasn't having it – and told Billy to kill him.'

'Sounds like Dan was a complete control freak,' says Mum. 'And yet he could be so charming . . .'

PC Hunt nods solemnly. 'Billy is not the brightest lad around. Dan had him wrapped round his finger. Billy admits that he panicked after stabbing Ryan and went running to Dan, who took the knife and said he'd deal with it. He must've been visiting Sarah and took the opportunity to stash it in your garden. We've charged Dan with conspiracy to murder.'

'I'm just glad you've got him,' says Mum, 'and Billy too.'

'Jemma,' says PC Hunt. 'I'm sorry I didn't believe you. I was wrong.'

I am shocked. He actually means it.

'But you didn't give up – you were determined to prove your theory right. And you did! We'll do our best to make sure Dan and Billy are both locked up for a long time. I hope you can forgive me, Jemma.'

I am stunned. I don't know what to say. His eyes look desperate now, pleading with me to let him off the hook. I didn't think he cared, but now I believe he does.

'OK,' I sniff.

'Thank you,' he says, his shoulders sinking with clear relief. 'That means a lot.'

54

I've realised something important. Being able to communicate doesn't mean that anyone's going to listen. The one thing I didn't want to happen is happening and there is nothing I can say to stop it.

'I know you're upset that I'm leaving,' Sarah sighs. 'And . . . look, I want to be honest with you. What's happened – it's changed everything for me. I'm sorry, Jemma, but it's only fair to tell you – I don't think I'm going to be coming back to work here.'

Out of the corner of my eye I glimpse the dark shapes of her cases in the hall. She's already said goodbye to Finn, though I don't think he has any idea what's going on.

'It's not easy for me and I know it must be very upsetting for you,' Sarah continues, 'especially after you rescued me so brilliantly!'

'YES,' I sniff.

'I want to explain. I want you to understand,' she

tells me. 'I haven't changed the way I feel about you. I still care about you. I still love you, Jemma.'

'GET BETTER COME BACK,' I sniff.

Sarah shakes her head. She looks like she's going to cry. 'It's just that . . . what's happened, it's made me realise . . . I've been hiding here in a way. This isn't actually my family, though I've kind of been pretending that it was.'

She wipes a tear from her eye. 'One day I'd like to have my own family and maybe be a foster parent like Lorraine. I think being here has been an excuse to not grow up – and what's happened these last few weeks has made me grow up – fast. Do you understand, Jemma?'

Of course I do. What she's saying does make sense. I've just been fighting it. I want her to stay so much. I don't reply.

'And maybe,' she continues, 'it's not so good for you to be so dependent on me. I know you need care, but other carers might be just as good or better – or different anyway, and give you different experiences.'

I'd love to tell her about Rosie. I don't want other carers, even though Sheralyn's been OK. I want Sarah.

'I don't want to stop you growing up and experiencing new things. And this sniff controller – it's amazing! It's going to change your life completely. You will have so much more control.'

I know she's right – you can't always keep things the same. I think about Jodi – new experiences can be good. I think about my future now I can communicate, all the possibilities. But . . .

'Tell me you understand. Please?'

Part of me wants to – but the rest of me refuses. I know it's selfish, but I want her to stay.

She strokes my hand. She looks at the sniff-controller screen – but I am not sniffing.

Then she looks at me and I see the pain in her face. She has been through so much. Suddenly I see I am hurting her and I don't want to do that.

'Please, Jemma?'

Sarah waits patiently while I sniff each letter.

'YES,' I sniff. 'LOVE YOU SARAH.'

Then as she hears the words spoken, she leans forward to hug me as best she can. I feel the wetness of her face as she kisses my cheek. I am crying too.

She lets go. The she gets a tissue and gently wipes my eyes. 'I'll keep in touch, Jemma, I promise. Your dad says you'll be able to text and email with this thing. It'll be great!'

She gives me her warmest smile and walks towards the door.

'BYE SARAH,' I sniff.

And she has gone.

55

Nine months later

I'm being pushed in my wheelchair and I am surrounded by people. I have never seen so many people and they all seem so tall and so close I feel like me and my chair are going to disappear under the crowd – flattened on the pavement. I'm trying not to be scared.

My new carer Alice is pushing me. I was anxious before she started, but I was surprised to find I actually liked her straight away. I had wanted it to be just me and Jodi, but the good thing is that, as Alice is pushing me, Jodi can walk beside me. Now and then she squeezes my hand. I catch the glint of her midnight-blue nail polish and look with pleasure at my own matching nails. I think of Sarah – that day when she did my nails, the awful things that followed. It feels so long ago now.

I didn't realise it would be so far. We seem to go

on and on. I'm glad it's not raining.

'I cannot *believe* we're really here!' says Jodi.

I've talked so much to Jodi. We meet up every weekend. Mum and Dad decided not to take a break from fostering, to my relief. They asked me if I'd like to go to Carlstone College in a few years' time and I do. Mum's finding out about applying for a place, but I don't know if I'll get funding. In the meantime I've started going to a mainstream school for part of the week. I was really nervous, but Jodi encouraged me to try it. I wanted to go to her school, but the council said a nearer one was more suitable. So I tried it – and I love it! It's not easy, but I have a teaching assistant to help me and everything is so interesting. At first I was doing two days a week there and now I'm doing three.

I have new communication software and I've had lots of training with a speech therapist who specialises in AAC. She's been brilliant and now I can select words and phrases from categories rather than spelling everything out. It's still very slow, but faster than typing each letter. I know it will take time, but I want to do my exams and go to university – just like Jodi plans to do.

I am also going on a sailing trip for teenagers with disabilities. Alice loves watersports and she told me she used to help on sailing holidays as a volunteer. I searched the Internet using my sniff controller and I found out more about it myself, and I've already been on a day's sailing course. It was amazing! Beats the local park, any day.

And Olivia came home! Mum and Dad were keen to have her and I told the social workers I wanted to give Olivia a chance too. It was weird how much I missed her in the weeks she was away. Her social worker has organised some therapy for her. She's a bit quieter than she was, but not much, and she still has tantrums. She talks to me sometimes, though, and it's wonderful to be able to talk back. She's still going to ballet lessons too. Olivia never explained why she took the money. She said she 'didn't know' and 'just wanted it'.

Finn seemed happier when Olivia came back. He is doing better, though it's not always easy to tell with him. He hasn't done any head-banging for months, at least. Mum hopes one day that he'll be able to communicate too.

I've had a few emails from Sarah. She's still living

with her sister and she says they're getting on really well. I miss her, but I'm glad – because I have my sister and Sarah is with hers too. She finally split up with Richard. I hope she'll find someone who will be right for her one day.

Next month is Dan's court case for kidnapping her. He's pleading not guilty, but the police have plenty of evidence against him. Dan and Billy's case for Ryan's murder will be soon too. They may show my video in court. If they do it will be the first time someone has given evidence using a sniff controller.

I suddenly realise we have arrived. This place is massive! Jodi is speaking to someone who's wearing a hat and looks like he works here. She's pointing to my wheelchair and asking which way to go.

We go up in a lift. First stop is the disabled toilets. Now we are back with Jodi and searching for the way through. So many people!

Jodi leads the way through an entrance labelled *Block C* and Alice pushes me quickly after her. We're at the front of a balcony in a wheelchair space with seats either side. I can't believe how vast this place is. It's a huge oval shape and I can see rows and rows of people below and across the other side who look as small as insects!

'You OK, Jemma?' Alice asks, moving round to face me.

'Thirsty. Please can I have a drink?' I sniff.

Alice reads the words as they appear and I don't bother to press the speaker. It is so noisy in here that I don't think she'd hear – even with the volume on full.

'Of course,' says Alice. She rummages in the bag for my drink and opens it. It's taken a while, but I'm getting used to being able to ask for what I want.

Once I've had a drink, Alice gently puts small earplugs in my ears. 'No!' I sniff. I am worried I won't hear properly.

'You'll need them!' Alice tells me and Jodi nods in agreement.

'Seriously, Jemma. It's SO loud!' she warns me.

'Exciting!' I sniff.

Jodi smiles back.

Then suddenly – there they are. They look so small on that faraway stage, but the screens are big so I can see their faces clearly. Glowlight! It is really them. I see Leo! My heart thuds. He is gorgeous.

The music starts. It is like a musical thunderstorm.

The beat is so loud and the vibration so strong I can feel it in every bone of my body. Then the voices. It is so loud – so incredible. I sing along in my head. I catch a glimpse of Jodi's ecstatic face. She squeezes my hand.

I am here at a Glowlight concert with my sister.

She is glowing.

I am alight!

AUTHOR'S NOTE

When I began to write this book, I had not decided how Jemma was going to be able communicate, although I knew she would need to by the end! Advances in technology have made communication possible for many more disabled people. However, there are lots of people who do not have access to this technology or are unable to use it for various reasons.

The device that Jemma uses in the book is inspired by a real invention, developed by researchers at the Weizmann Institute. Trials have shown that some severely disabled people and people with locked-in syndrome, for whom other systems have not worked, have been able to use this device. And as a relatively inexpensive product it has the potential to make AAC technology accessible for more people than ever before. It has not yet gone into production, but my hope is that by raising awareness, this book may help to persuade a company to take this up and make it commercially available. I dream that one day everyone who has the potential to communicate will have access to the equipment they need.

ACKNOWLEDGEMENTS

Firstly, I would like to thank my lovely agent Anne Clark. I couldn't ask for a better agent and your commitment to this book has been wonderful. I am so lucky too to have brilliant editors in Stella Paskins and Liz Bankes at Egmont. Your skillful editing, enthusiasm and excitement about the book has been amazing. Thank you to the whole team at Egmont!

I am eternally grateful to all those people who took the time to answer my questions, and to read the manuscript and give feedback at various stages. Any errors are my own and not the fault of anyone acknowledged here.

For help with cerebral palsy and AAC information I am especially grateful to Jonathan Kaye, Ellie Simpson of CP Teens, and Debbie Simpson, Natasha Bello, Julie Bello and Kate McCallum from 1Voice, Kate Caryer from Communication Matters and Unspoken Theatre, and Jenny Herd from Communication Matters. Thanks also to Carl Ritchie, Joan Ritchie and Kevin Robinson who answered police related questions for me.

From the Weizmann Institute I would like to thank Lee Sela and Noam Sobel for answering many questions about their recently developed communication device.

I would not be the writer I am without the fabulous City Lit where I started out as a student and now teach. From there I formed my own Friday writing workshop, with talented writers Jo Barnes, Angela Kanter, Vivien Boyes and Derek Rhodes. Your constructive criticism and support has meant so much to me. I'd also like to thank my young adult beta readers, including those found for me by Janis Inwood, librarian at Southgate School, where I was educated, and Jessica Pliskin whose excellent suggestion really helped.

My family – every one of you, I thank you for your support – and especially my husband Adam for all his love and for putting up with my mind being elsewhere a lot of the time (and for his helpful suggestion, gratefully received and ignored, that I should write about zombies). Final thanks go to our children Michael and Zoe, to whom this book is dedicated. I know you are annoyed at not being old enough to read it yet – but you will be, one day, and I enjoy watching you grow so, so much.